Other books by Marc Pietrzykowski

...and the whole time I was quite happy (poetry)

The Logic of Clouds (poetry)

Following Ghosts Upriver (poetry)

visit the author virtually at www.marcpski.com

MUSIC BOX DANCER

BY MARC PIETRZYKOWSKI

Music Box Dancer

Copyright © 2012 by Marc Pietrzykowski

Cover by: Marc Pietrzykowski
Cover Photo by: Waynerd
Back Cover Photo by: Nicole Capoccitti

ISBN-13: 978-0-615-65239-9
ISBN-10: 0-615-65239-5

visit the author virtually:
www.marcpski.com

Printed in U.S.A

with love and gratitude to Ashley

and thanks to Dolores for all the smiles

CHAPTER 1

The first time everything changed for Charlie Price, it happened suddenly, an explosion: the earth cracked and split, the dishes leaped off the shelves, strangers on the street accused him out of the corners of their eyes. The second time, the change snuck up on him: just a noise, a small, cheap, tinkling noise that burrowed its way up through the summer air, burrowed through the sweating window pane, and finally burrowed its way into Charlie's ear. Once the noise made it that far, it grew wings, but still, it was little more than a tiny buzz at the fringe of his concentration, though he could not rouse himself enough to swat it away, could only wave his hand distractedly beside his ear. He was too perfectly comfortable to bother, his chair exactly attenuated to his body, his blanket snug, his bones folded just so, and as he turned the page, Mary Frances Kennedy Fisher moved from Aix to Marseilles, which was the most exciting thing that had happened to him in at least three days. Then several more neurons blazed to life, and he heard the song, and he recognized it for what it was: goddammit, he thought, it's dark outside, fully dark, it's well past dusk, and the ice-cream man's little tape-looped song is still playing. Now the earworm had him, his equilibrium was ruined, his comfort gone, the warmth of the chair starting to cloy. Past dark on a Thursday night, and he's still playing that fucking song, what is it, "Turkey In The Straw"? I guess he could be counting his money, Charlie reasoned, laying the book down open on his chest and taking a sip of flat ginger-ale. But why does he need the song to count his money? Does it help him focus? What an asshole, he decided, sliding the glass back onto the shelf beside his chair and ejecting himself in a single, stiff-legged motion, the green blanket sliding to the ground. He walked to the window and peeped between the curtains: yes, the ice cream man was directly in front of his house, parked, tiny loudspeakers on its roof squealing at a remarkable volume. The driver was hidden from view, and Charlie imagined him warty, squat, balding in patches, of indeterminate ethnicity, a member of the tribe of trolls that once were their own species but had long ago bred with every human race on the planet, and with some non-human ones as well, because they were trolls and that's what they did, when not hiding under bridges or eating babies. Why, he could be luring children to his truck under the cover of darkness, hoping to snatch one or two and puree them, mold them into bomb pops and nutty buddies and choco tacos! The thought was nearly enough to push Charlie into his shoes, set him marching out to confront the troglodyte and his wheedling abduction machine, but just as his resolve congealed, the truck drifted away from the curb and down the street, its song dwindling away toward downtown. Ah well, he thought, another chance at heroism slips through my fingers, time to get ready for work.

He hadn't slept all day, and was not getting nearly enough sleep these days, Charlie knew—his mother told him so, often, almost robotically—but working third shift can do strange things to your biorhythms, strange and sometimes wonderful things. Not that any wonderful things had happened yet, 6 months into the job, but the potential was there. The job itself was certainly not wonderful, and becoming a denizen of the dark (like the trolls!), being wide awake when most of the workaday world was asleep, then trying to sleep himself while everyone else made coffee and money and daiquiris and love, that was not so wonderful either, though it did give his disdain for other people a much keener edge. He gnawed his lip and fretted about REM states and the clowns who ran the world and sat at the edge of the toilet and pulled on his left sock, but it was not his, he noticed too late, it was Emily's, it barely fit over his foot. He sat with his ankle resting on his knee and stared at the distended sock. He thought he had gotten all her things together and taken them to her mother's house, there weren't many bags at all, 4 or 5 black plastic trash bags stuffed full and tied neatly at the top. Bonnie, Emily's mother, wasn't at home, so he'd left the bags on the front porch. They were too black, they sucked light into them, he drove away thinking he'd left an event horizon on Bonnie's porch. He hoped she didn't fall into it accidentally. She may well have, he'd heard nothing from any of Emily's family since the funeral. It was a very cold day, he remembered, even for Late January, very cold and very dry, snow squeaking underfoot, the kind of cold where the wind crowded into your lungs like it was trying to hide from an even colder wind behind it. The people were all cold and stiff too, the whole affair would have been totally antiseptic had the minister not kept sneezing every few minutes, and if the wind had not suddenly picked up and whipped everyone's coats and hair about just as they began lowering her into the ground.

I must send the minister a thank you card, Charlie thought, and pulled Emily's other sock onto his right foot, distending that one as well. He walked on the pads of his feet out to the kitchen and stood on first one foot, then the other, while pulling his boots on and zipping them up at the sides. Tomorrow was his day off, he realized, a thought that filled him with an uneasy mix of angst and resignation. Another evening spent trying to take over the world... The heat slapped him out of his doldrums even before he'd made it down the stairs: the air conditioning did not, unfortunately, work in the hallway. It was he that paid the electric bill, after all, surely his landlord would see his way to running some duct work out there; what was his landlord's name again? Gandalf? Gundam? Charlie could picture his wide, pocky, Middle-eastern face, or maybe he was Pakistani, or maybe—and then the heat swallowed him, and Charlie gasped. It was late June, and already far too hot even for the first big bloat of summer, things were not right with the planet at all, it was plain for anyone to see, to feel, the earth was gagging and retching and probably getting ready to spit up. He made a slithery sort of dash for his truck, slid into the cab, started it, and threw on the air conditioning, causing a fart of warm, oily air to spurt out onto his knuckles. The moon was nearly full as Charlie pulled into the street, shaking his head at the fools wandering up and down the sidewalk, uncovered, oblivious to the danger draped over them like a moldy tarp.

Charlie worked, in the most minimal sense of the word, as the overnight security guard at a re-purposed drive chain factory that now made both solar panels and aromatherapy products: candles, lotions, sachets, and other olfactory baubles. Most of the employees went back and forth between the two sections of the factory, depending on which side needed more workers, and there was rarely enough work for a third shift, so Charlie generally only had to interact with Jerry, the morning guard who replaced Charlie when his shift was over and who said little, but who always mentioned the Bible when he did speak; Ella, who ran the aromatherapy business and tended to stay at work late pretending to be a buxom 18 year old on internet chat rooms; and Frank, the B-shift guard, who was usually sober enough to stay awake when Charlie arrived at 11:30. He also had the rare and unpleasant occasion to talk briefly with Al, his boss, who ran the security agency and so took it upon himself to drop in unannounced at various job sites to be sure everything was "on the up and up." Al didn't try to be unpleasant, he just mistook his over-bearing manner for charisma, thinking the cringing, uncomfortable reactions he usually got from most everyone signalled delight in his presence. He was the kind of person who still pinched other men's nipples and yelled "titty twister!", even though he was well into his fifth decade on the planet, and he was, in a limited way, the bane of Charlie's existence.

Everyone needs a bane, of course, if only for balance, and so Charlie took the presence of Al's yellow Hummer beside the guard shack in stride. He'd always thought Al's truck looked medieval, and he pictured tin hatted soldiers poking crossbows out the slitted windows at him as he parked and soaked up a last bit of air conditioning. I'm glad Al drives this stupid machine, at least I know someone who has one, he thought; they come hulking by on the highway, inhuman, insulting, it helps to think there's a human being inside, and it helps even more that it's Al. As he threw open the door and eased out into the yard, the heat swallowed him whole, began to smother him, his head fizzled, his heart spun like a child trapped in a revolving door. He made it to the steps of the guard trailer and burned himself on the door handle. Jesus, it's not *that* hot: he stared at his hand, it was a deeper red than Al's truck, and then it grew darker, blackening at the edges, bits of skin turning to ash, floating upwards like there was a campfire at the end of his arm. "Hey, Professor!" Al bellowed from the open door of the trailer and snapped Charlie out of his trance. He looked at Al, then at his hand again, which looked the same as it always had: a bit doughy, short in the fingers, except for the ring fingers of either hand, which were longer than the middle ones. "Come on, letting the air out," Al yelled again, and gestured with a fat sweep of his own hand to come inside.

Frank was in the trailer, sitting bolt upright behind the grey metal desk that held keys and fobs for the guard's walk-arounds, a stack of *Penthouse* magazines from the 1970's, whatever magazines Charlie left there, and little else (he rarely brought books to work, he would get absorbed and forget to do his rounds). Frank's hands gripped the edge of the chair to steady himself, and Charlie knew if he moved to switch places and take the guard's chair, Frank would fall off and spill onto the floor, so instead he stood just inside the door, bending his head slightly to accommodate the low ceiling. Al did not need to bend down; he was short and bulbous, made of furry skeins of skin draped one atop the other like a stack of pancakes. He wore a gold earring in one ear, a rope of gold around his neck that let a gold cross nest in a plume of white chest hair, and a gold and ruby pinky ring on his left hand. He slapped Charlie in a way he thought playful with his undecorated hand, coating the side of his face with a mix of herbal moisturizer, Axe body spray, and tiny clumps of dried insta-tan. "How ya doin', Professor? Getting any?"

Charlie shifted his weight to the other foot and watched Frank's face turn purple. "No, Al, not getting any."

"Too bad, young guy like you? But maybe you come across too smart? Yeah," Al squeezed Charlie's bicep suddenly, "chicks like the muscles, you know? Not big brains like you got. You should come to the gym with me sometime. It's air-conditioned... I bet you spend all your time on the computer games and never even go out with a girl. Or a guy, what do I know!" he let out a chuckle with the last comment and nodded at Frank, letting him share the joke. Frank's grin stayed plastered to his face, a small bubble of spit forming in the corner of his mouth.

"Yeah, well, you know I hate the heat, and I got other things going on now, so,—"

"Other things? What else is there besides gettin' some? Am I right Frank?" Frank nodded his head in a slow oval, and even managed to bark out a laugh. "Ah well, anyway, just thought I'd come by and see howzit going, we got a new guy starting in the morning,

Billy'll be down to show him the ropes so you got nothing to worry about, Professor. Just thought I'd tell ya so you don't go and shoot him." Al laughed again, and Frank started coughing along. None of the guards at the site carried guns, there was nothing to steal, so Al liked to ride them about it, thinking one of them might rise to the challenge and go get his pistol permit, thereby allowing Al to raise his rates. Then again, none of them knew that Al didn't have a gun, was in fact scared of guns, and that his closest experience with a firearm was naming the cat he found in the alley behind his apartment "Luger," because it was a very dark, almost metallic grey, and because he already had a cat named "Petunia."

"Ok. What happened to Jerry?" Charlie asked.

"What happened? How the fuck should I know what happened? He quit, that's what happened, and if he thinks he's gonna work in Security anywhere in the state of Pennsylvania ever again, he's got another thing coming." Al hitched up his pants, and Charlie wondered why he tended to curse more the longer he stood in the trailer. Maybe he just had to get comfortable. "Alright, keep your business in your britches..." Charlie and Frank both stared at Al, waiting for him to finish the rhyme. "In your britches..." They continued staring, silent, until Al punched the door open and finished on the way down the stairs: "and your wheels between the ditches," and continued muttering all the way to the door of the Hummer.

"Ok Frank, time to go home," Charlie said.

Frank sagged. "God, I want to bite that guy," he said, swayed upwards, sat back down in the chair, then lurched decisively into a more-or-less standing position and teetered toward the door.

"Yeah, but then you'd get all greasy," Charlie replied, and Frank made a small gagging noise that made his cheeks balloon out. He swallowed and called out, "have a good one" to Charlie as he tipped himself down the steps toward his car and, eventually, the apartment he shared with his older brother, Dennis, who had become obsessed with model trains after falling from a roof 17 years earlier. Frank spent most of his time at home sleeping or apologizing for stumbling into some spectacularly complex train setup that had appeared in their narrow living room while he slept.

Charlie settled in behind the desk and stared at the interior of the trailer. The only other furnishings, aside from the desk, were a locked filing cabinet that Al said was there when he took over the contract and which no one had ever succeeded in opening; a Miller Lite-themed mirror; a coat rack, naked in the summer; and a wooden crate filled with bits of junk, mostly broken key boxes of the sort that the guards were required to turn every few hours as they did their rounds. There were 7 key boxes on the site, which was probably 6 more than were needed, but Charlie actually liked doing the rounds, only one box was outside the factory proper, so the heat wasn't too terrible and he got some exercise. But really, he told himself, this thing with the heat is a problem I'll have to face sooner or later, shit, I was hallucinating earlier, he thought, I was full-on hallucinating like a Siberian shaman. But what can I do? Go back to the therapist Mom found for me, Mr. Nadu, a nice little man but utterly useless, or maybe I'm just not trying very hard but then why should I try hard, or at all, I'm traumatized and have every right to be, I held my fiancee in my lap while she died on the kitchen floor. That gives me some right to be fucked up, yes? I deserve it, yes? PTSD is ok by me. If my hand appears to turn black and ashy, so what, maybe tonight I will see demons, big winged things all made of fire, flying around my head. Or maybe I just didn't get enough sleep. He hoisted his feet up, threw them on the desk, and wondered why they felt so mealy in his boots, then remembered he still had Emily's socks on, and started to cry.

The new security guard was also named Al, a detail Charlie believed was all the reason boss Al needed to hired him. Al the younger was wiry and carbuncular and his spine was slightly bent, so that even though he was clearly in his late teens, he also looked ageless in the way of Scotch-Irish sharecroppers. Charlie managed to escape without speaking much to him since Billy, Al's tightly wound assistant, arrived just before shift change to train him. Train him, yes, that's what they call it, Charlie mused, teach him all the arcane knowledge, the looking alert, the smiling vacantly, the clipboard thwacking; he felt wry and tired and apprehensive all at once, and he was beginning to dread the terrible gap in his calendar: his nights off work. As he drove, he catalogued the books he needed to finish over the next few days: *Anna Karenina*, which he was not as wonderful as he'd expected; *The Mind Parasites*, which was perfectly terrible, and thank God he was nearly done with it; and *Two Towns in Provence*, which had actually helped him re-learn how to enjoy eating once in a while. There were a couple dozen others waiting to be read, all stuffed in the big bookshelf he and Emily had bought at the Salvation Army and then dutifully filled, hunting together in crooked used bookstores. They even took a bookstore tour one very long weekend, driving almost four hundred miles from small town to hamlet to back alley, following a map of bookstores Charlie had assembled, carefully avoiding anything like a chain or big box store, eating several crappy diner meals and one truly splendid one, staying at a no-name Motel somewhere near the coast, near enough to smell the ocean, but only just—and so, Charlie had enough books to make it through his "weekend," through many weekends, in fact, and when he had read all the books on the bookshelf, well, then he would be better, he would be healed, the feeling of stepping carefully lest he fall through the earth into an abyss would fade away, yes, he would walk more steadily and Emily's face would remain but would frame and hang itself in his mind somewhere cherished but unobtrusive. Maybe I can feel it happening already, he thought; I can sleep for six hours at a stretch now, sometimes, and I am eating again, and I even make coffee and shave and I am actually reading the books, not just swimming in the pages, and once the books are done, I will figure out what to do with this life, and it might be good and it might not but—he looked up and realized he was sitting in his driveway, truck still running, with no recollection of his drive home. It was 8:45 in the morning, and the sun was beginning to roar.

To make it through the days he wasn't working (and he thought often how funny it was that his work helped him persevere, since all he did was sit at a desk in a trailer and listen to the radio and read very old magazines and take a walk every two hours, but damned it if didn't help somehow), he had tried to reenact his routine from home, sat at his kitchen table in his guard shirt and took a walk around the neighborhood every two hours, but it just made him feel stupid, and he completed the experiment by trying to light the VFW hall on fire with some kitchen matches, so no more role playing. Instead, he developed another routine, one tailored to his home and the things within, and it involved sorting the books he was going to read on the table beside the recliner in three piles of three books each, drinking warm, usually flat ginger ale, and, sometime around 3 a.m., heating and eating a frozen pizza. After he had completed a book, he put an "X" beside its title on a list he had printed out when he first hit on the idea of reading them all, and then he would go and get the next book from the shelf and put it at the bottom of the appropriate pile. On days he worked, he would read from 7 p.m. until it was time to leave, and so he was, after three months of reading, more than halfway through the contents of the bookshelf.

He usually began his day-off reading routine at 5 p.m. or so, after a few hours of spastic sleep in the recliner; the bed was not a place he had been able to breach yet, and so it sat, unmade, un-slept-in, still full of odors and grit. To lull himself to sleep, he would turn the television on and turn the sound down until it was loud enough to hear but not loud enough that he could understand what the noises meant, program it to go off in an hour, and cocoon the mottled green blanket around himself. And so it was the Thursday morning the new guard started working, the TV down low, the cocooning process begun, when the phone beeped. It could only be his mother, no one else ever called him. He knew she would let the phone beep 13 times, hang up, and call back, continuing this way until he answered, so he sighed and let the blanket slip off onto the floor. On his way to answer the phone, walking past the bedroom, he saw someone standing by the bed and let out an audible squawk, then saw it was his own reflection in the bedroom mirror. How many times had he jumped at his reflection? Jesus, was this still the day after Emily collapsed on his lap in the kitchen, was she still asleep there on the bed, he had only to go wake her... He stared at himself in the mirror, at his narrow, bony head, his sunken cheeks and almond-shaped eyes drawn down at the corners; he recognized himself as a stranger at an airport recognizes someone they'd flown with a week ago, someone notable without any solid reason to be so. As he stared, the phone stopped beeping, and the walls hung dully in the mirror behind his head. Then the phone began beeping again, and he went into the kitchen and lifted it from its cradle. "Hi Mom," he said, as he always did, since it bothered her that he had no need to say "Hello."

"Oh Charlie, stop that. Answer the phone like a person." Her voice quavered habitually, and she cleared her throat when she was done talking to signal to the other person it was their turn to respond.

"I'm answering like the kind of person who knows when their Mom is calling them, because she calls at the same time, every two days, lets the phone ring thirteen times—"

"Ok mister smart guy, I get it. Did you eat breakfast?" Charlie sighed.

"Yes Mom, at 9:30 last night."

"You know what I mean. Did you eat this morning! That is what I mean. Did you eat when you came home?" Charlie sighed again, prompting his mother to continue. "And stop sighing like that! Someone needs to check on you, stop acting like I'm killing you, I'm not killing you, I'm checking to be sure you're eating regularly. You're a stick, you need to eat, not be a stick."

"I ate, Mom. I ate a lot of waffles and now I'm really sleepy, actually."

"That's good, I'm not sure I believe you, but that's good." Charlie heard her muffle the phone against her body and yell "shut up and sit down!" at someone, presumably Otto, her boyfriend Grady's pit bull terrier. Or it could have been Grady, he supposed.

"Mom, thanks for calling, I'm really tired now."

"Did you go to school and register yet?" she asked.

"No, not yet." He stifled another sigh.

"Charlie Price, you need to get your butt down to that school and register, you only have three more classes to graduate. Really, I mean—three classes!" Her voice had been sliding upward in register, and she caught herself and dropped it down to a level she considered gentle and comforting. "Do you need anything? Grady is going down to get a load of gravel, I can have him stop by, pick up something at the store for you?"

"No Mom, I'm set. Just gonna go to sleep and then do some reading tonight," he answered. Now it was her turn to sigh.

"Alright baby, you call me if you need anything."

"Ok Mom, love you."

"Love you too."

Charlie dropped the phone back in its charger and looked out the kitchen window at the brown brick wall of the building beside his. There were two black-framed rectangular windows set in the wall at each floor, six windows in all with a door set between the bottom two, a pleasing orderliness of larger rectangles contrasting with the smaller bricks... He had never spoken to any of the people on the other side of the windows, though Emily had, and his mother had, when she first visited them in the new house they'd rented and he'd bitched about how late she was and how all his goddamn life he had to be the responsible one and Emily looked out the window and broke his rant, "there she is," and they both looked out and saw his mother hugging a small, round, dark woman in the doorway between the lowest of the two windows. She said the woman had been one of her students at Perry school, third grade, Ms. Price, the hippie teacher who built an idea of what a mother should be and stuck to that idea with a sweet desperation. He couldn't really fault her for it and did so anyway, he was only three or four when his father got in the blue Buick and disappeared into the back story, and with no family to fall back on—her ultra-orthodox Lebanese parents had already disowned her for marrying a red-blooded American hill-billy—Miriam Lahout Price had to improvise a new identity, one that could laugh drunkenly in the middle of a Pennsylvania winter, whip up a casserole for the PTA picnic, and slap her son into shape with the same hand that wiped his cheek free of the tears her slaps provoked. In any case, she'd given him a model of what not to be: an impersonation, a person who lived to one side of themselves, always checking that her role was being played adequately, but never so well that she ever crossed the line and betrayed the scene with sincerity. Emily liked her. Charlie liked her too, but never really knew her, and the small round woman who'd been her student had moved out shortly after the two of them hugged in the doorway; Charlie and Emily watched as she came home and found her furniture piled on the lawn, disappeared for several hours, and returned with a panel truck and five or six Latino guys in sleeveless shirts. Charlie had to stop Emily from going to help them, they were supposed to go to a barbecue and didn't have time, they were in charge of fruity drinks and had to get the blender in the car and all the cans of juice were starting to thaw. He ended up getting very drunk at the barbecue and falling off the back deck, and Emily drove him home and told him the next day that he spent most of the night begging to go next door and help the neighbors move, and she kept telling him they were already gone, and he would nod and then forget and start begging again.

CHAPTER 2

The rain began just as Charlie was finishing *Anna Karenina*, just as Levin was leaning out on the terrace, watching a storm drift by in the distance; in fact, Charlie heard the first drops fall just as Levin heard distant drops falling in the lindens, and the synchronicity scared him and gave him a headache, so he fetched some ibuprofen from the bathroom, swallowed it, and went back to the novel. After more than 300 pages, the character of Levin had finally worked its way into Charlie's head, and his prickly speculative voice had become interesting, even gripping. "What am I about? To me individually, to my heart has been revealed a knowledge beyond all doubt, and unattainable by reason, and here I am obstinately trying to express that knowledge in reason and words…" yes, Charlie thought, to be possessed of such a drive to understand, to find meaning, that would be wonderful, perhaps that is what I think will come at the end of my reading project, a new desire welling up inside me… As his reverie slackened, he heard another noise snaking its way between the rain drops, a tinny, creaky sounding noise that he recognized as the same song that had irritated him late the night before: the ice-cream truck must be parked in front of his house again, and not only was it night, it was raining as well. Charlie stood and drew back the curtain, and sure enough, the ice-cream truck was parked by the curb, running lights on, loudspeakers fully engaged in littering the neighborhood with the insipid song."Goddammit,"Charlie thought, and went to the kitchen and pulled on his shoes. He was nearly done! Two or three more pages of dour Russian soul-searching and he could put an "X" next to another title on the list! He dashed through the kitchen door and down the stairs and out to the yard; the steamy heat nearly knocked him down, but if Konstantin Dmitrievitch Levin could find his way to God, then surely Charlie Price could make it across 12 feet of neglected grass to the curb. And make it he did, sweat mixing with the light rain that was still falling. He touched the truck lightly to make sure it was real, then went around back and looked in the driver's side window.

The driver was not a troll, nor did he seem the descendant of a troll, but instead was a vaguely handsome, dark haired young man with a high forehead, a jutting nose and weak chin. He was hunched slightly, apparently studying something in his lap. A small light on the interior of the cab shone dirtily, and Charlie saw that the driver's hair looked wet, slicked back and up in a pompadour, like one of the guys from the movie *Grease*. Charlie banged on the side of the truck near the passenger-side window, causing the greaser to start and turn his head first away from the sound, then back toward Charlie, his small eyes narrowing to slits. "Hey!" Charlie tried to bark at him, but it sounded more like a cough, and the man only continued to stare. "Hey, would you turn off the loudspeakers?" Charlie continued, "people are trying to read, you know? Like, in peace and quiet? So, turn it off, please?" The intensity of the man's stare made the end of Charlie's plea trail off into a whisper, and he continued to stare for a full minute before turning away and reaching toward the passenger's side. Charlie smiled and stared at his shoes and had begun to mumble "thanks" when he lifted his head and noticed that the ice-cream man was now pointing a pistol at him. The world tilted, as though one of the legs holding up the camera recording the scene before him had suddenly shortened, and Charlie nearly toppled over backwards. "Fuck off, now," the man said quietly.

"But why are you—"

"Fuck off now, chief," he repeated, "I'm having a really bad day."

Charlie began to back away, into the middle of the street. He looked to either side, there were no cars approaching, no people walking in or out of the apartment building, no one riding their bicycle up to the middle school to play basketball. The rain started to fall more heavily, and Charlie felt the opposite curb strike his foot. He sat heavily on the curb and kept watching the man, who had returned to whatever it was he was doing in his lap. He was soaked, and sat with his elbows around his knees, rocking gently. A knot grew tight in his stomach, grew clenched like a fist and drew energy from the rest of his body to feed itself, leaving Charlies' arms and legs and head too weak to move, except to keep rocking, kneading the ball in his belly, peeking up from time to time at the driver's head, just visible above the window frame. After a time, the man finished what he was doing in his lap, lifted a flask from somewhere beneath Charlies' view and took a long pull from it, screwed the top on, and then started the truck's engine. He put his arm on the edge of the open window, looked at Charlie once more, said "pussy" just loud enough for Charlie to hear, and pulled away from the curb. The ball in Charlie's stomach suddenly exploded, sending bits of venom into each of his limbs; he stood, or someone stood, Charlie knew it was his body but he was elsewhere, watching his body from behind glass, watching as the body stood, picked an egg-sized rock from the road, and threw it at the back of the truck, where it thunked loudly against the door and caused the truck's brake lights to come on. Charlie's body froze, saw the driver lean out and point the gun at it, then ran across the street and up the lawn as the truck reversed, squealing. He heard the gunshot just as he reached the corner of the house. He continued around the corner, up the stairs and through the kitchen in what seemed a single motion, finally falling in a heap behind the recliner. He could hear the truck idling at the curb, and then the ice-cream man was yelling up at his window, "I'm going to fucking get you, chief, I know where your house is." Charlie started to cry. He cried as he heard the truck drive away, and kept crying as the rain gradually stopped, and the crickets began to sing. He never used to cry, not since he was a child. He didn't even cry much as a child, not that he remembered. Most of his childhood memories were short, random scenes that meant little to him: peeling a hard-boiled egg at a picnic table, tasting the wet sand under the jungle gym, his mother—or some other woman, the harder he tried to recall her face, the less he could remember it—coming through the kitchen door with a severe new haircut; his mother's best friend Marcia playing cards and whistling off-key. Nothing about crying, though he felt sure he must have, even though his life held nothing altogether too tragic or even untoward, just the usual Western PA childhood bullshit, nothing to suggest he would become a man who cried every other day.

Then again, he never planned on holding his fiance in his arms while she dribbled black bile out of the corner of her mouth. There was no class for that in any school, not any he went to. When he was in sixth grade, one of his schoolmates had drowned in the pool, and even though Charlie barely knew the boy, he had to go to the school counselor for grief therapy. She was a tiny woman with a huge head, and when she smiled, her lips got smaller instead of larger, which made her head look even larger. She sat across from him in a regular school chair, and a low table covered with plush toys sat between them. She asked how he felt, and he said fine, and she asked if he missed his friend Brandon and he said no, and she smiled her little smile and said, "not even just a little bit?" Charlie remembered that childhood scene well enough because that was the moment he realized part of what it was to be an adult, that he had to lie and say yes, he felt terrible, he really really missed him, and if he didn't, he would have to keep coming back to see the big-headed counselor until he did. Other kids had bar mitzvahs, or sneaked booze out their parents' liquor cabinets, or went to work, or had their parents give them "the talk" when they were on the lip of adulthood, and this event served the same function in Charlie's personal time-line, his first moment of adult consciousness, the moment that he learned that adults lie to one another constantly, and do so willingly, because if they stopped, the whole world would crumble.

And really, why not? Lies are not the cause of pain, lying badly is the cause, a lie that breaks and reveals itself. Words are lies, of course, everyone knew that, but even our vision, what our noses smell, everything that comes in through our senses is a lie as soon as we realize we have sensed it, we take the raw stuff—the bus going by, the particles of scent floating up from a rose—and make it into another bullshit story with no end, a thing that is not a thing, a representation... Jesus, I sound like that philosophy professor whose class Emily and I took together, the one whose breath was so bad you could smell it in the back row, but he sure did know his shit. He was right, there is no connection, we make a galaxy of lies and get mad when someone is not so good at lying, when God is suddenly a question and love is suddenly a question and even my actual presence, the thoughts in my head, questions, unanswerable questions that make us tell lies and are in fact lies themselves. It's not phony, like Holden Caulfield might say, it's how we survive, there is nothing that is not phony, its just more lies all the way down till you've peeled the whole damn onion. And then, if you are still alive, you start crying. Charlie grabbed an arm of the recliner and hoisted himself up, leaned over, and looked at the notebook. The middle column listed *Anna Karenina,* then *The Martian Chronicles.* Great, he'd seen that on TV already. Should be quick, anyhow. But first, some asshole just shot at me. He shot at me, people usually call the police when someone shoots at them, shouldn't they even be here already? He dialed 911 and told the woman he'd been shot at, no, he was fine, yes, he could meet the police and show them where the shooting took place, right in front of his house.

The cops were both men, and looked so much like lovers it made Charlie feel a little silly. One was a head taller than his partner, both wore small, black mustaches, and both bent their bodies the same way as they stood, listening to Charlie tell them what happened. They even finished each other's sentences. Charlie showed them where the ice cream truck had been parked, and where the bullet had struck the siding and torn off a chunk of the corner. He even remembered the license plate of the truck, to his surprise. "No one living downstairs?" the taller man asked, peering through a window while his partner searched the ground nearby for a slug.

"No, not for 2 months. The landlord isn't here much, I don't know," Charlie mumbled.

"That's lucky," tall cop said, "someone could have gotten hurt."

Short cop wandered back and looked again at the spot where the bullet hit the building. "I can't find the slug, it could have ricocheted just about anywheres." He had a trace of southern drawl, and his eyes were nearly black.

"Ok, well, let's go radio it in," tall cop replied, and the two men headed back to the car. Charlie stood in front of the house and looked up and down the street: it was just after 4 a.m., and the streetlights gave off a sickly yellow glow that made the sidewalks look even emptier than they were, feverish and abandoned. I shouldn't have called the police, Charlie thought, and gnawed his lower lip. They won't find anything, they won't do anything, and I'm sure the neighbors are looking and thinking I'm some meth head, up all hours and gunshots and... both cops emerged from the patrol car and walked slowly to where Charlie was gnawing. "What do you do, Mr. Price?" tall cop asked, tilting his head expectantly.

"Do? I'm a security guard, I work for Top Gun Security, down at Collins Place. I work the night shift, why?"

"Have you had dealings with Mr. Cavuto before tonight?"

"Cavuto? Is that the guy who shot at me? No, I didn't even know his name 'til you just told me." Charlie began to shift his weight from side to side.

"Never bought an ice cream?" short cop asked with a smirk.

"What? No, I never bought an ice cream from him." Charlie felt his face getting hot.

"Never bought anything else?" tall cop said; short cop added, "from Cavuto?" and they both crossed their arms on their chests at the same time.

"No, I told you, I never heard of him, I never bought ice cream from him. He shot at me, remember? What's this all about?"

The two men shared a glance, then tall cop raised an eyebrow and turned back to Charlie.

"It seems strange to Officer Forrest and I that someone would fire a gun at another someone, and that that someone would have no idea why, and that they would wait six hours to call the police. That seems strange. Does it seem strange to you?"

"Yes, and I told you, all I did was ask him to turn off the music, and I waited because I was scared."

Then it was short cop's turn to speak: "It sure sounds like that ain't much of a reason to shoot at someone, Mr. Price. But then again, Mr. Cavuto might be a particular sort of person, the kind of person that people like you should avoid. Do you understand me?"

"I-I don't think I do, what do you mean avoid him?" Charlie struggled.

"Avoid him means stay away from him. Don't talk to him," tall cop said, "don't tell him to turn off the music, don't buy ice cream from him, if you see him on the street don't make eye contact, if you see him in a bar, don't buy him a beer. Stay the fuck away from him. Now do you understand me?"

Charlie scratched his forehead. "So, somebody shot a gun at me, tried to kill me, and you tell me to stay away from him? That's it?"

"That's the best advice you'll get this week, I promise you that. There are, as I'm sure you know, being in the security field and all, serious people in this world. Serious people that you should avoid. If you really never met Mr. Cavuto before, then just trust what I'm telling you, and if you do already know him, then you know what I'm telling you is the truth. Stay the fuck away from him, and if his ice cream is too loud for you, get some earplugs." With that, tall cop turned and began walking back to the cruiser.

"You have a good night, now," short cop said, and turned to follow his partner. Charlie watched them climb inside, then realized his mouth was hanging open, and that he had to pee. He hadn't felt so confused in quite a while, so deliberately fucked with, and it made him feel both energetic and off-kilter. I've been messed up for a few months now, he thought, but I'm not letting these assholes get away with this, I'm not going back in my hole. I hope he comes and plays his little ice cream song under my window again, I hope he does. But he has a gun, he shot at me, and the cops—the cops!—told me not to mess with this guy, that's pretty severe, but I can't do nothing, I can't... I've come too far to crawl back in now.

He went up the stairs to the bedroom, opened the closet door, and pulled out a laptop computer, thereby breaking one of his first rules: no internet, no television, until all the books are read. But I have to break the rule, he told himself, I have to find out who this guy is, sometimes the rules have to be changed or the whole game could crumble. Is it a game? He sat at the kitchen table and plugged in the laptop's power cord. Am I just playing a stupid fucking game, pretending it will help me get over Emily? What happens after I've read all those books? Will I be a happy little person? Go back and finish school, get a job in a cube farm some where, find another girl who looks a little like Emily but not too much, have a few kids, take them to tee ball and ballet, retire and buy a fishing boat... somehow, I don't think that's likely. Everything is different now, like I remember people saying after the planes hit the World Trade Center, "everything is different, on 9/11 everything changed"— didn't seem different to me, the crazy people got a little crazier, the stupid people a whole lot more loud; senior year of high school, all those kids going around trying to convince each other this was the most important thing that ever happened in their lives, out here in rural Pennsylvania, hugging in the hallways and crying and all those goddamn pep rallies, the principal and the teachers trying to look serious and sincere, flag decals and ribbons sprouting everywhere like dandelions. What a joke. Now, if you lived in New York, if your mom or husband or daughter never came home that day, then yes, everything was different after that day, but for everyone at home watching on TV, making it more than just another remotely viewed tragedy required a whole lot of work. When there's an earthquake in Peru and a whole village dies, does everything change for people watching CNN in Idaho? What about when a drone missile goes astray and kills a family at a wedding in Peshawar? Everything different now? The laptop was asking Charlie for a password, and he realized he no longer had an internet connection, he'd canceled it when he started reading. It was almost 5:30, so McDonald's would be just opening, and they had free wifi. And coffee. Shitty coffee, but he hadn't slept in nearly 24 hours, and the walls were starting wiggle.

The phone began ringing as Charlie turned the key in his front door lock. It was late for his mother to be calling, and she'd already called yesterday. He threw the door open, slung the laptop across the kitchen table, and yanked the phone out of its cradle. "Mom?" he blurted.

"Charlie, hi, no, not your Mom," a male voice answered, followed by a chuckle. "It's Greg, how ya doin'?"

"Oh, Greg, sorry. Fine, thanks, just fine." Charlie felt like he was talking far too quickly, like his mouth was fluttering somewhere to the left of his head, a hummingbird darting.

"Whatcha been up to, man? How's life?" Greg had moved to Pearson to attend the state college, graduated a year before Charlie was supposed to, then decided to stay after his girlfriend's father gave him a job running a sporting goods store. He liked to drink beer and play his guitar, and he was considered quite skilled at the beer-drinking part. He was also a womanizer, and he owed Charlie money, and he was, well, fake, he couldn't help it. Greg said "Hey, Mo's birthday is next Saturday, we're having a barbecue, you think you can make it?" Mo, that's right, Maureen, a broad, strong woman with large teeth and a low, rumbling laugh, so much more than Greg deserved.

"Oh, uh, yeah, maybe, well I've got some stuff—"

"Come on, she'd really like to see you, me too. A few folks from D-wing will be there, Kyle and Chidsey and Eric, and Sarah, and we'll have some beers and I'm gonna cook burgers and stuff."

The names Greg recited fell out of the phone like old coins, talismans of a lost tribe, scraps of newsprint. Charlie was suddenly occupied by the past, by the time before Everything Changed, images and sounds and sensations came at him from all directions but at a strange remove, as though he were overhearing someone else's story and could not turn away. Eric getting punched in the face by his Dad after winning at darts. Greg asking to borrow Charlie's truck again and taking off to Philly for 3 days, Greg throwing hot dog buns at everyone and starting a small scale food fight, Kyle picking his nose, which he did unashamedly, claiming it was a form of rebellion, challenging social conventions. And Emily, telling Kyle that was bullshit, picking your nose in public was just gross.

"Um...well," the slitted eyes of the ice cream man suddenly appeared in Charlie's head, staring at his friends, staring at Emily, sneering at Charlie. "Yeah, ok, I can come by for a while. What time?"

"Really? Cool, I'll start the grill around 3, so just, you know, get here when you get here. Kick ass, man, see you then?"

"Can I bring anything?"

"No, no, just whatever. Bring some beer if you want," Greg muffled the phone and spoke to someone else. "Yeah, just beer, but we'll have some here too, so just come."

"Ok. Thanks Greg."

"Later."

Well shit, Charlie thought, I guess I really am getting better. He looked around the kitchen, his gaze lighting upon the faint stain on the floor near the sink where Emily had drooled bile from her mouth as he held her. He had tried to clean it up but he couldn't get completely rid of the stain, though to be fair, he hadn't scrubbed all that hard. He took his blood and bile spattered clothes into the backyard and burned them in a barrel the same day he scrubbed the floor, and the day after that, he went and got a job at Top Gun Security. Things change, we move on, I'm part of that cliche but it really is true, and now look at me, I'm going to a party. Hell, I left McDonald's and it was already 80 degrees out and I was fine, sweating, sure, but I didn't feel like I was going to crawl out of my skin, didn't hallucinate any birds swooping at my head or my hands charring black. His internet search for Cavuto proved fruitless, but he did manage to survey some news sites and check his email, which seemed to have become a spam cesspool. The news aggregators spat strange headlines at him: there were still wars going on in Iraq and Afghanistan, Bush and Cheney were still grotesque pricks, the bird flu was still scaring people, everyone seemed to have forgotten about Abu Ghraib because Reagan died, though Charlie felt sure he'd died years earlier, John Kerry was apparently the Democrat's great white dope. Immersing himself in the empty calorie gush of media made him feel secure, even as he loathed his own appetite; he knew that this loathing was the source of the feeling of security, that he needed to be actively spiteful about mass culture if he were ever to feel better about himself—and oh how he loathed that language, "feeling better about myself," as though he were two different people, the self and the other self that looks on and gauges and judges. It was utterly vapid and yet strangely delicious, the way the language crept into him, the way he allowed himself to be shaped by messages and messengers he held in contempt, all so he could feel his disgust more keenly. His disgust was reminding him who he was, how he lived; his loathing was helping him get better. He sat all morning in a McDonald's, drinking coffee that tasted like water stirred with a crayon, watching the breakfast rush come and go. A group of retirees sat in one corner on plastic benches and chairs, loading their terrible coffee with sugar and cream, pontificating about the same nonsense Charlie was reading about on his laptop, even using the same terminology, while the tables near the front were reserved, it seemed, for folks on the go: hospital orderlies, construction workers, landscapers, and the odd businessman in a suit and tie, pecking at his blackberry. At 9 or so, a gaggle of teenagers came in and colonized the dining room, causing the retirees to contract slightly, inching closer together and lowering the volume of their speechifying to a low mumble. By 10, the restaurant was empty, and Charlie watched an elderly woman in a crooked McDonald's hat drag a mop around the sticky vinyl floor. The whole spectacle, the parade of fools, the trapped-animal stench, had nauseated him, and as he got in his truck, he realized he hadn't felt so good in months.

And now, to top it off, he was going to a party. .

CHAPTER 3

Al the younger was late again, he'd been late every day since he was hired, including the first one. It was 8:45, and Charlie's shift ended at 8. Normally he didn't much care, but then again, normally Al was 15 or twenty minutes late, not three quarters of an hour late, and Charlie didn't want to get stuck working his shift, it was the first time he'd looked forward to the weekend since he started the job and pulling a double was not how he'd envisioned it. He lay the completed crossword puzzle on the desk and looked out the trailer window. The Dominican guys who did the day shift at the solar panel shop had arrived a few minutes earlier, and Ella had opened the aromatherapy storefront at 7 to let the let Rakim, her delivery man and brother-in-law, start filling his van with reeking boxes of product. And no Al. The last thing Charlie wanted to do was call Al the elder, since he would just beg Charlie to work in his place, but he couldn't see a way around it, so he dialed his bosses' number and crossed his fingers.

"Hello, Top Gun Security," Al answered.

"Hi Al, it's Charlie Price at Collins Place."

"Charlie, what the fuck? Talking on the phone on company time?" Charlie grimaced. He knew if Al were standing in the trailer, Charlie would be expected to smile. Thank God for phones.

"Yeah, I guess I am. Your new guy is late again, really late. I'm thinking he isn't gonna show."

"Sure he is," Al answered. "Don't worry, he'll be there in a minute."

"Are you sure? How do you know?"

"Cause he's with me. We're just pulling in."

Charlie went to the window and looked out. Sure enough, Al's H2 was just pulling into the lot, and sure enough, Al the younger hopped out of the passenger seat and clambered down, then turned and smacked himself in the ass in the general direction of Al the elder, still sitting in the driver's seat. Charlie wondered if he'd made this last bit up. Did he really just see this kid slap his ass at Al? The door to the trailer swung open and Al bounced in. He was a twitchy one, for sure, wiry and constantly wiggling like a seedling in the wind. Charlie was very grateful he'd never been trapped in an elevator with either Al.

"Hi Professor, sorry I'm late!" Al was also a compulsive giggler, and several small titters escaped during the course of his brief salutation.

"That's ok. Hey Al?" Charlie asked.

"Yeah?" Al was already arranging himself behind the desk, laying a GameBoy and a copy of *Guns and Ammo* on the desktop and unlacing his shoes. Charlie wanted to ask him why he slapped his ass at Al, why he was being driven to work by Al, just exactly what the fuck was going on, but decided that it was really none of his business, as long as young Al showed up for work.

"Nothing, never mind."

"Uh-huh. Got a big weekend planned?"

"Actually yeah, I'm going to a friend's birthday party"

"Woo-hoo, don't do anything I wouldn't do!" Al winked. Did he really wink? Did he really slap his ass? Charlie's ears began to ring.

"Ok, I won't," he said, and went out to his truck. After two days of scorching heat, the temperature had suddenly dropped, and a light morning breeze blew across the yard. He drove slowly, through the rusting monochrome of the industrial section, through the remains of downtown, through the student housing and fraternity section, before finally pulling into the lot in front of his house, not quite in the worst part of town, not quite in the student section, a secluded little polyp of buildings bounded by the rail yard on one side, Veteran's Park on another, and the highway on a third. He pulled into the driveway and saw a strange car parked in the spot beside his, a brown Audi of indeterminate age. As he unlocked the bottom door, he heard voices on the other side of the stairway and remembered that the Audi belonged to his landlord, Gundal, Gural, something Patel. The door to the lower apartment swung open and Charlie resisted a ferocious urge to launch himself up the stairs, lock the door behind him, and hide under the bed. He turned toward the open doorway and watched the goddess Kali emerge from the apartment, bright red tongue flicking in and out of her mouth, hips swaying, necklace of severed heads swinging between her breasts. One of her arms thrust what appeared to be Charlie's own head toward him, and she began to hiss his name, drawing out the syllables: "Chaaarrr-lieeeeee, Chaaarrr-lieeeeee." Charlie blinked and shook his head and Kali vanished, leaving a small man and an even smaller, very dark-skinned woman standing in her place. "Charlie? Are you alright?" the Indian man asked.

"Wha-, yes, sorry, hi Mr. Patel, sorry, I'm very tired."

"Ho, I guess so, always working. Charlie works the night shift, and studies all day," he said, turning his head to reassure to the woman. She nodded, but looked at him skeptically. Charlie decided this skepticism was a permanent feature of her face.

"Charlie, this is Mrs. Clarke, she is interested perhaps in the lower unit," he continued, then turned back toward the woman again. "Mr. Price, who we call Charlie, is a very good tenant. He is very quiet, he has no loud parties or plays loud music, he always pays on time, hard worker...."

"Mm-hmm," Mrs. Clarke answered. "He look a little craven to me."

"Ah, craven, yes, I don't know that expression, what does it mean?" Mr. Patel asked.

"It mean he want tings, but don' know what to do when he get'em."

"Oh no," Mr. Patel wrung his hands, "Charlie is not a greedy man, Charlie is a good Hindu, yes Charlie?" Mr. Patel laughed, Charlie coughed, and Mrs. Clarke shook her head.

"Craven puppy," she said. If Charlie or Mr. Patel had known her when she was a much younger woman, when she worked for her father, who supplied guns to much of Kingston in the early 1980's—if they had watched her remove the top of a man's head with a machete because he tried to rape her younger sister—well, they would have agreed Charlie was craven and then maybe made her a batch of cookies and rubbed her feet.

"I'm not, well, whatever, I'm really not greedy, I just like to read and stuff. I have to go, I'm really tired," Charlie blurted, and started up the stairs.

"Ok, Charlie, you get some sleep. Oh yes, I forgot, Charlie?" Mr. Patel called up the stairs.

"Yes?" Charlie replied.

"Someone did put a hole in my siding?"

"A hole?"

"Yes, come I will show you. I will be back in one quick moment, Mrs. Clarke." Mr. Patel led Charlie outside to where the ice cream man's bullet had scabbed a small chunk out of the corner of the house.

"Oh, that. Yes, as a matter of fact..." Charlie told him the whole story, the shooting, the police coming by, and what they had said, though he left out the part about throwing a rock at the truck.

"They know this man and they don't arrest him? He shoots my house and the police do nothing?"

"I know, I thought it was pretty weird. They even told me his name was Cavuto, and that I should just stay away from him."

"Cavuto?" Mr. Patel rubbed his chin and his eyes flared slightly with recognition. "Oh yes, I think I know this name. Yes, I definitely know this name," he said, and began walking back to the house.

"You know him?"

"I know his name," Mr. Patel called over his shoulder. "I think you should, this time, listen to the police, Charlie."

Charlie woke at two in the afternoon in a terror. He had no idea where he was, the sun was shining on his face, a phone was beeping, and his skin was thick with sweat. Then the flotsam of his life came flooding back: who he was, where he was, his social security number, Emily brushing back her hair from her forehead, Al slapping his ass at Al, the smell and the giggles when he'd peed himself in first grade, watching silently as his mother buried their one and only dog, apprehension and confusion at the idea of going to a party after 8 months of near-hermitage, and the need to get up and answer the phone. "Hello?"

"Charlie, oh Charlie, you're home." It was his mother, and she was crying.

"Yeah Mom, what's wrong?"

"Oh, I'm sorry to bother you. It's—" she collapsed into unintelligible sobs.

"Mom, calm down, I can't understand you."

"It's Grady, he's gone, he left me! Oh Charlie, I'm all alone!" Charlie winced. He didn't see much future with her and Grady in the first place, and the fact that his mother didn't consider her son part of the equation that ended with her being "all alone" irked him.

"Take a deep breath, Mom," he said, switching the phone to his other ear. "Tell me what happened."

"What happened? I wish I could! Nothing! I don't know!" Her voice was getting louder. "I went to work yesterday, and came home and he was gone, and all his clothes were gone and Otto was gone and Otto's food and, and there's a note on the table, and all it says is 'sorry'. Sorry! Sorry for what?"

"I don't know Mom," he said. His mother let out a community theater-sized sigh.

"I know you don't Charlie, I'm sorry. I'm just frustrated, that's all. He just, well, he seemed different."

By "different," Charlie understood her to mean that Grady seemed like a man who would not leave her. Of the nine boyfriends she'd had in the years since Charlie's father had left, all but one had left her suddenly and with little explanation. Vince, the only companion who had offered a detailed explanation had decided he was gay, and wanted to still be friends, but then later decided he was not in fact gay, got married to a much younger woman, began producing offspring, and subsequently no longer wanted to be friends.

"He seemed like a doofus, Mom."

"Oh don't say that, Charlie! Well, yes, I guess he was kind of a doofus. Do people still say 'doofus'?"

"I just did."

"Yes, but you're different, Charlie."

By "different," Charlie this time understood her to mean that he was an odd duck, a weirdo, a peculiar person who was free to indulge his peculiarities because his mother decided it was ok to do so. This did not, contrary to her intent, ever make him feel any better or more comfortable about his peculiarities.

"Ok, well, you want me to come over?" he asked.

"No, no, I mean, if you want to... but, ah, could you do me a favor, Charlie?"

"What, Mom?"

"Well..." this hesitancy does not bode well, Charlie thought. "Do you think, you work in security, do you think you could go to Grady's, you remember where Grady's shop is, right, and see if he's there? I don't want you to talk to him or anything—"

"Mom," Charlie interjected.

"Just see if he's there, please? I just want to know if he's there, and I won't bother you anymore and I won't go looking for him, I just want to know."

"Ok Mom, yes, I'll go look."

His mother's voice grew small and girlish: "Thank you Charlie. I love you. Will you go today?"

"Yes, Mom, love you too," he said, and turned off his phone. Jesus, no wonder he was such a mess. He sat at the kitchen table and looked across at the calendar on the wall. It featured pictures from the Philadelphia Museum of Art, and was opened to November 2003. "Thanksgiving Mom's House" was written on it in red, in Emily's hand. He stood up and tore it from the wall and stuffed it into the garbage can, which he noticed was overflowing with frozen pizza boxes.

Grady was a big-bellied, light-skinned black man who kept his hair very short and wore a small pencil mustache. The mustache was evidence of a certain fastidiousness, or at least a pretension to fastidiousness, and it's presence on Grady's lip was irritating to Charlie, since he was familiar enough with Grady's habits to know he was a sloppy person. The coveralls he was currently wearing, for example, were stained with the usual oil and grime mechanics attract, but also with mustard and some kind of crusty white substance, and his chests pockets hung unzipped.

"Hey there Charlie, your Momma send you to fetch me?" Grady asked, without looking down from the underside of the car he was servicing.

"Well, Grady, you could've done more than left her a note. She just asked me to come be sure you were still around. I guess she's worried about you."

"Don't need to worry about me, I'm good," he said, and let a wrench clang onto the work bench beside him. He wiped his hands on his coveralls and looked at Charlie. "What else you need?"

"Nothing, just came to see if you were here, that's all she asked me to do."

"Well you seen me, and you can tell her I ain't coming back, don't even try."

"Ok, I'll tell her," Charlie answered. Grady inhaled deeply and squinted at Charlie. It was his conviction that Charlie was largely worthless, lost in his own head like so many of the white boys he'd known in Vietnam. They were the glory boys, the ones who volunteered and came over looking to be heroes, or at least find a sense of purpose buried somewhere in a rice paddy. Grady spent three tours in 'Nam, and never saw a bit of combat. He volunteered for whatever menial duty no one else wanted, digging latrines, washing dishes, anything to keep himself alive, and as a result, his memories of Vietnam were of a beautiful country, blue skies, clear water, excellent reefer, cheap pussy, and hard, stupid work. He considered the years he spent there the best of his life.

"So, you alright?" he asked, since Charlie had not made a move to go.

"Yeah, I'm fine. How's Clovina?" Clovina was Grady's daughter, she'd spent time in jail for kiting checks before finding Jesus.

"She good, she's working at the library now."

"Oh, nice, the library."

As Charlie stood and looked at his shoes, not sure what else to say, or how to say goodbye for what he assumed would be the last time, a car pulled up behind him and honked, making him jump. Grady looked up, annoyed, then stood up straighter and walked quickly past Charlie into the lot. He looked almost scared, Charlie thought, and turned to see a man getting out of a late model, powder blue Mercedes Benz. "Hello, hello, sir," Grady called, and shook the man's hand. They talked briefly, too quietly for Charlie to hear, and then Grady turned and walked into the back of the shop. The man he'd been talking to was facing the other way, looking out to the street, and then he turned back and Charlie saw it was the man who'd shot at him. He looked at Charlie without interest. "Hiya chief," he said, and smiled on one side of his face. It was not a welcoming smile. Charlie nodded, and looked back down at his shoes.

Grady came out of the back with an envelope and handed it to the ice cream man and shook his hand again. He gave Charlie one more half smile as he bent his head down to get in the car, then backed out and drove away. Grady watched the car until it turned out of view, before finally remembering Charlie was still standing in the garage. "You still here?" he barked, and went quickly to his workbench, where he fuddled with assorted tools.

"You know that guy?" Charlie asked.

"Do it look like I know him?"

"Yeah," Charlie paused and waited for Grady to look up at him again. "He drives an ice cream truck, and he shot at me last night." Grady's lower lip twitched slightly.

"What? What'd he shoot at you for?"

"I told him to turn the music off, the ice cream truck music. It was dark and he was just sitting there, letting the music play."

"Goddamn, Charlie. Some people you got to know not to fuck with," Grady said, and shook his head.

"That's what the cops said."

"You called the cops?"

"Well yeah, he shot at me." Grady snorted incredulously, and walked over to where Charlie stood. He stared down at him for a minute, close enough for Charlie to smell cheap cologne and french fries and motor oil.

"I don't care if he burn your house down. He's a bad man, and his whole family's bad, and you just stay away from him. What you say he was driving, an ice cream truck?"

"Well, he was parked in it, I didn't actually see him selling ice cream or anything. But he had the music on."

"You promise me you see that man coming down the street, in a ice cream truck or a dump truck or that Benz or on foot, you see him coming you go the other way. You promise."

"Sure, I promise," Charlie said, and both men knew he was lying.

"Tell your Momma I ain't coming back, tell her I got somebody new."

"Do you?" Charlie asked.

"Sure I do," Grady said, and both men knew he was lying.

CHAPTER 4

The night before Mo's birthday party, Charlie found it difficult to read. He'd left Grady at the garage and went home and slept hard, harder than he had in a long time, and he again woke disoriented, sweating, and stuck to his chair. He had blown through *The Martian Chronicles*, managed to kill off *The Mind Parasites*, and had finished *Two Towns in Provence*, so he added fresh books to the bottom of each pile on the table, and then checked the title of the topmost books with his list: *The Erection Set*, by Mickey Spillane; *Invisible Man*, Ralph Ellison, which he was sure he'd read in college; and something called *The Little Book Of Fishing*. He was glad Emily had taken so much time sorting through the books at each place they'd stopped, looking for good ones, or at least interesting ones, rather than just filling the bookcase with James Clavell and old typing textbooks. She was attentive to detail that way, and she hated being wasteful: she wanted books she and Charlie would actually read, and he cringed remembering the argument they'd had in one of the last bookstores they found, when he'd decided he'd had enough and was bored with the whole project and why didn't she just grab a boxful and sort them out later and give what she didn't want to the Goodwill. That was the end of their book-buying trip, they drove the next 4 hours in total silence. They'd lived together for two months at that point, and it was the first time Charlie saw her fall like a pebble into a mood so dark and so bottomless there was no sound anywhere around her, nothing he could do would lift her out, no lines could be thrown down for her to climb out, or even to simply tug and let him know she was still alive. I should have figured it out, he thought; I should have paid more attention and learned how to make her more comfortable, how to send a few sparks down into her cave. Her mother just wanted her to go back on Xanax or whatever, God she was a witch, Emily hated the fake feeling of meds, said it made her feel like she was stuck behind a soapy window.

Charlie shook his head violently and opened *The Erection Set.* The dedication read: "FOR SHERRI... whose part in this book can hardly be denied. Elaborated on, certainly, but a pleasure to research, peruse, and enjoy. Doll, you are magnificent!" Doll. When was this written? 1972, and there was a half-naked, no, a fully naked woman on the cover holding a pistol, with a banner declaring "over 1,500,000 copies in print!" covering her breasts. Emily loved cheesy detective novels. Charlie flipped absentmindedly to the final page, and read the last paragraphs:

"...but he shouldn't have said it the second time, enjoying the scene of naked flesh, part soft and part hard, wondering where to put the bullet, because where a .45 hits you it tears one hell of a hole and the .45 was right next to my hand and the first shot took his arm off and the second left no memory of Arnold Bell's face in anybody's mind because he had no face to remember. His skin and bones were indented on the wall behind the headless body and tomorrow I'd have to get another crew out here to clean up and patch the hole and if I were lucky, the quarts of blood wouldn't flow through the cracks in the floor and ruin the ceiling downstairs.

"Now?" I asked her.

The two shots were still reverberating in her ears. She looked at the mess by the door and didn't get sick at all. She didn't hear me, but she knew what I said.

Sharon smiled and turned the old brass ring around so it looked like a cheap wedding band. "Shut up and fuck me," she said, "like a dog."

Holy crap, I better start at the beginning, Charlie said to himself. She is indeed magnificent, or does magnificent mean something like "scary as hell?" He looked up and out through the gap in the curtains, picturing the ice cream man pulling up to the curb and leaping out, pistol in each hand blazing, while Charlie returned fire from behind his truck. He saw a bullet spin the man around by the shoulder, saw his face smeared with blood while Charlie dragged his body upstairs, tied him to a chair, and woke him by throwing bleach in his face and in his wound. "Why don't you fuck off now, CHIEF!" Charlie yelled, and he knew that he had really yelled it, he was not imagining that part. He took a sip of water and tried to go back to his book, read the first few sentences several times without comprehending them, and gave up.

The toaster oven plinked and Charlie went into the kitchen to get his pizza. His two pizzas, actually, he'd decided to try the mini-pizzas since they fit in the toaster oven and because they looked even more vile and tasteless than the regular sized ones. He lowered the oven door, pulled out the tray, and let out a shriek as he dropped the tray and the pizzas on the linoleum. His hand was throbbing and he stared at it, watched as it start to turn red, began to bubble and even steam a little. The pain was searing, but he could not move toward the sink or freezer; the pain was the center of the universe, and everything—the house, the city of Pearson, the planet, the Milky Way the endlessly expanding galaxy—all hovered, waiting, tethered to the tips of Charlie's fingers and palm. He belched abruptly and the spell was broken, so he turned on the cold water at the sink and plunged his burnt hand into the stream. Fuck, all I wanted to do was try a different kind of pizza, I can't even manage that, he whined at himself. Will I know any people at this party? Sure I will, but I don't really want to see anyone, I won't laugh when Kyle tells some stupid dirty joke or pours beer down the front of his shorts, or my shorts, more likely. I like Greg and Mo but they just want to stare at me, I'm the freak with the dead fiance. Maybe I should fling poo like the monkeys at the zoo, let them stare, let them stare. But then Kyle would think it was funny and he would fling his shit around too. He reached back across his chest with his left hand and turned off the tap, then opened the freezer and pulled out an ice tray, which he whacked on the table until several popped loose. He bundled them up sloppily in a dish rag and grabbed the bundle with his right hand and sat down at the kitchen table. The clock on the microwave read 1:35. The next time he looked, it read 3:20, and his burned hand rested on a soggy dishrag, in a puddle of melted ice cubes on the table.

Having wasted most of the night, Charlie decided he'd better spend all of Saturday, and all of Saturday night, getting caught up with his reading. There is a point to this, after all, he told himself; *I am trying to get over this thing that came and took over my body and the only way to kill it is by sticking to the plan.* He ignored the phone the first time it rang that morning, but remembered the next time it rang about Grady and his Mom so he answered it, and Greg asked him to stop and get some ice and of course he said yes because he was a coward, he couldn't say no, what was he supposed to say, *I can't come because there is a demon in me that must be exorcised by the reading of second hand books? Shit shit shit.* How did Greg get his land line anyway, he'd thrown the cell phone away and, he thought, only given the house phone number to his Mother and the landlord. He would ask him: *hey Greg, hey Mo, Happy Birthday, how did you get my unlisted number anyway?* His hand hurt. His leg hurt too, and he didn't remember doing anything terrible to that. Oh stop crying, he barked aloud, and the front door and toaster oven and refrigerator snickered in response. *Ok, I imagined that, appliances don't snicker, I'm just stressing, it's just a party, a party with people I know and who must like me a little, why else would they invite me. A party with people I know, people who know what happened and there, that's the problem, back to the beginning again.*

He stopped at the Pump'n'Pantry and bought a six pack of Pabst Blue Ribbon and a bag of ice and drove on to Greg's house. Greg and Mo lived at the other edge of the factory zone, in what had been a suburb when the steel mills thrived, and now was a buffer between the city and the suburbs proper. Half a dozen cars were parked along the street and in the driveway, and Charlie went past and continued around the block, chewing on the inside of his lip. The third time around, he went past the house and parked along the curb fifty feet or so from the next nearest car. He hoisted the ice over his left shoulder and grabbed the six pack with his sore hand, let out a grunt, and shifted the ice to the right shoulder so he could steady it with his right hand and carry the beer with his left. The ice felt good on his shoulder, it was starting to get pretty hot out and making it hard to breathe, and it really felt good on his hand. He started up the driveway and heard voices and music coming from the backyard, so he went around the corner of the house and was promptly poked in the groin by a huge furry nose. "Charlie! Lester, No!" A lazy, staggered chorus of greeting echoed out of the small group gathered in the backyard as Mo came running over to pull the head of an especially broad Newfie out of Charlie's crotch. "Hi, oh god, I'm so sorry, he does this to everyone," Mo said, looking down and straining helplessly at the dog collar. Greg appeared at her side and also started tugging, whereupon Lester suddenly seemed to remember he had business elsewhere and galloped away to throw himself into a plastic wading pool. "Hey man, great, glad you could come," Greg said, and slapped Charlie on the shoulder. Greg had wavy, dark blonde hair and a short, sandy beard, and was good-looking the way people who aren't quite beautiful tend to be: nonthreatening, casual, nothing out of place but nothing especially notable. Charlie had long thought the beard, and other facial hair experiments, were attempts at making something interesting happen on Greg's face, but in fact each new goatee or soul patch or set of mutton chops only reinforced the bland acceptability of the rest of his head.

"You look good, how are you?" Mo asked, and Charlie remembered that she had the rare genius of actually meaning it when she asked how you were. She was tall and sturdy looking, and had a face that was almost the inverse of Greg's: not exactly what you would call attractive, but interesting, even compelling, and certainly not homely. Her eyes were set far apart, her nose was turned up and high on her face, and her jaw was broad and filled with large teeth, which she had long since given up trying to hide.

"I'm fine, you know, working, doing a lot of reading, the usual. When did you get the dog?"

"Ha, it was my bro's, he had to go overseas. And what exactly is 'the usual'?" Greg raised his eyebrows. "I heard you were working as a security guard."

"Yeah, over at Collins Place."

"Where? Where is that?" Mo asked. Charlie explained where it was, and they nodded.

"So that's usual? I would've thought you'd be working in DC by now, keeping some congressman in line, or in grad school or something."

"Nah. The whole poli-sci thing was kind of boring, really. I don't even know why I majored in it, just seemed like the thing to do." The three of them began wandering toward the small half-circle of people and lawn chairs that faced the grill, and beyond that, a soccer field and a junior high school.

"So you got your paper, though?" Greg asked.

"Greg stop, he just got here," Mo said.

"No," Charlie sighed, "didn't graduate yet. I'll get around to it, I'm doing other stuff right now."

"Ok, right on, right on," Greg said, "hold that thought, I need to flip the burgers. And gimme that ice, thanks a lot for picking it up."

"He doesn't mean anything, he just wants to know you're ok," Mo said once Greg was out of earshot.

"I know, it's ok. Oh shit, Happy Birthday! I almost forgot."

"Yeah, thanks, it was actually on Thursday, but you know, who has a party on Thursday?" Mo answered, pulling a strand of hair behind her ear. Charlie looked out toward the soccer field.

"Here you go, happy late birthday," he said, and pointed the six pack in Mo's direction.

"Ah, thanks, my favorite," she laughed, and yanked out one of the cans.

"Hey Charlie, pull up a chair!" a high, throaty voice called to him.

"Hey Eric," he answered, sliding into a lawn chair, "hey Kyle, hey Sarah."

"Hey..." their voices competed for anonymity. Charlie sighed, pulled out a can of beer for himself, and offered the remains of the six pack to the rest of the group. Each shook their head no and held up their own bottles or cans to prove it.

"Hey Charlie, how many communists does it take to screw in a light bulb?" Eric asked in his squeaky voice. He had a narrow, high-browed head that was slightly bent in the middle, which made his mouth seem off center.

"None, the bulb contains the seeds of its own revolution," Charlie answered.

"Ha, he did poli-sci, dude, what you didn't think he'd know that one?" Kyle laughed.

"That's funny," Sarah said, and everyone sipped their beers at the same time.

Even the heat didn't bother Charlie, he barely noticed it, other than when he grazed his bad hand against the rough plastic arm of his chair. The sudden sting coursed up his arm and tightened the veins in his neck and he winced, his lungs constricting. But just at the point of anxiety, Kyle cracked open a beer that someone had shaken up, sending a geyser into his forehead and loosing a string of comic cursing and laughter from the assembled crowd, followed by a furious round of texting, presumably about Kyle's soggy head. By nightfall, Charlie was half-drunk and absolutely stuffed with cheeseburger and macaroni salad. Five more people arrived as the sun was setting, and three more as Greg switched on the porch lights and lit tiki torches. The various lights conspired to make the darkness strange, flickering, aquatic; bottles of tequila and vodka were cracked open, and joints were passed around. Charlie recognized most of the people who had arrived late, their faces familiar from school and parties and small town living. One heavily pierced and tattooed guy he recognized as a bartender from the Lumberyard, the largest college bar in Pearson, and he asked Mo who the guy was again, and if he still worked at the bar.

"Yes, that's Kiko, don't you remember? He's Sarah's brother," she replied.

"Oh yeah," Charlie answered, and took a pull on the joint Mo handed him. "I like his tatts."

"I know, they're pretty cool. I got a new one, want to see?"

"Sure," Charlie said, and Mo pulled the sleeve of her shirt up to reveal a freshly done image of the Queen of Hearts from Alice in Wonderland on Mo's shoulder.

"Oh wow, that's fucking great," Charlie said, and squinted closer, examining the detail.

"Yeah, thanks, Greg wasn't so crazy about it when I said that's what I wanted, but he likes it now."

"He should, that's cool."

"Hi Beth!" Mo shouted suddenly, and ran off to hug someone in the latest group of people coming around the corner of the house, laden with boxes of beer. Charlie watched her for a moment, then sat back in his chair. He blinked, and Mo was at his side again. "Charlie, this is Beth, Tony, and Ron," she said, gesturing at the three figures standing beside her with a practiced sweep of her hand. Mo had grown up on a dairy farm, and dreamed as a girl of being a professional hostess, guiding people through glamorous soirees the way a conductor led an orchestra. She also dreamt of being a fashion model, and an actress, and a wealthy heiress, anything that did not involve daily exposure to milk, cows, or cow shit.

Charlie nodded at the three newcomers: two very carefully, but casually, dressed men and a woman much less so. "Hello," said one of the men, Charlie though it was Ron but he'd already lost their names. She must be Beth, at least I've got that straight, he thought. And Beth must have heard his thought, as she promptly sat in a chair beside him and took a sip from a flask she drew out of the pocket of what seemed to be a pair of army-surplus cargo pants. She offered the flask to Charlie, who declined with a shake of his head. "I'm already pretty drunk as it is, thanks."

"You don't seem that drunk," Beth replied. Her voice had a sarcastic edge to it.

"Yeah, wait till I try to stand up," he laughed. Beth smiled and took another sip from the flask, then put it back in her pocket. Ron and Tony had vanished.

"Where are they all going?" Beth asked, looking out toward the soccer field. A group of a dozen or so people had left the party and were giggling their way across the grass, some waggling flashlights.

"Probably playing glow bocce."

"Explain."

"It's just regular bocce, except Greg has balls he painted with glow in the dark paint. He puts them under a light in the garage whenever they have a party, so they can store up some light, then they play bocce in the dark, I think they must have black light lamps out there too." Even as he spoke, they saw a small orb flit across the surface of the soccer field.

"That's an interesting idea," Beth said, "but they don't look glow in the dark, they're flickering."

They watched another ball slide across the field. She was right, it was flickering like an electric light.

"Huh, maybe he refined it," Charlie pondered.

They sat and watched the flickering balls clustered on the dark field, watched shadowy figures gather the balls up and toss them out into the darkness again, one by one.

"That is weirdly mesmerizing," Beth said after a time, and took a phone out of one of her pockets and began snapping pictures of the scene.

"Yeah, it really is."

"Or I'm really stoned."

"Or both," Charlie answered. Beth let out a short laugh.

"So what do you do for fun, Charlie?"

"Ah," Charlie felt her attention shift toward him, and he drew his feet under his chair; "lately I been reading a lot."

"No shit. Like what? What are you reading now?"

"Um, *Invisible Man*, and a detective novel, and a book about fishing."

"Do you fish?"

"No, just, uh—just reading essays about it. Some of them make it sound like fun, but I never went."

"What detective novel?" Beth asked, and lit a small, brown, plastic-tipped cigar.

"I—ha, I can't remember the title, but it's by Mickey Spillane. It's junk, but it's fun. I could probably finish 5 of his books before I'm done with *Invisible Man*."

"I loved that book when I first read it, back in high school, then I read it again for my comps and thought it was kind of, I dunno, kinda too much all at once, like some harder editing would make it less floppy," Beth said, chomping down on her cigar.

"Floppy?" Charlie puzzled.

"Yeah, floppy, like, he tries too hard to make everything really heavy, and that makes some parts, well, floppy, baggy, limp. Ever read *Juneteenth*?"

"No, that Ellison too?"

"Yes, and it's way floppy, but it's comfortable, like the floppiness was not an accident. I'd rather read James Wright, or Toni Morrison, if I'm feeling literary."

"I don't know either of them," Charlie admitted, and felt a strange flush of aggression in his chest. Beth stared at him, her mouth open.

"You never heard of Toni Morrison?"

"No," Charlie smiled. He wasn't sure why.

"*The Bluest Eye*? *Sula*? *Beloved*?"

"Nope, nope, nope."

"Well damn, Charlie, you better put some Toni M. in your reading list, yo!" Beth slapped her hands together and laughed. "I wrote a senior thesis on *Sula*. Great, great book."

"I'll have to find it, once I'm done with all the other ones on my list."

"Yeah, shit, I know what you mean. I finished my degree and thought, since now I'm really and truly unemployable, I'd have all this time to read, and all I do is find more books I want and put them in piles."

"Yes!" Charlie yelled, "I mean, me too, I have piles. What is your degree in?"

"English Lit," Beth said, and they both paused, then burst out laughing. "I mean, it seemed like a good idea at the time. It was a good idea, I learned so much, and I got to read all these great books, and I'm great at a very small part of Trivial Pursuit—there, see, I did it again," Beth sighed. "College is not about getting a job, you know? It's about learning stuff and finding out what you love and where you might want to go next and..." Charlie waited until her voice trailed off and her eyes turned inward.

"I only have three classes left, and I can't seem to do them, I just don't see the point," he said, and Beth turned and tilted her head quizzically. "It's like you said, college is for learning and, and, it's that part of your life, but now I'm past that part, I'm doing other stuff. You know?"

"Shit, man, if I quit with only three classes left my grandmother would slit my throat. But then she paid for tuition, so I really wouldn't blame her." She tossed the spent end of her cigarillo on the lawn and ground it out. Charlie looked at her nose, strong and pointed and graced by a small bump in the middle. She was, he realized, quite striking, and seemed to have devoted considerable time trying to disguise that fact. She felt his stare and looked back, smiling shyly as someone behind him yelled "Charleeeee!" He smiled back briefly, then turned in his chair.

"Whaaaat?"

"Come play spit!" Charlie shook his head. "No way, I hate that stupid game, and I gotta go to the bathroom," he said, and stood up for the first time in several hours. He teetered a bit.

"You ok there, captain?" Beth asked him.

50

"Yeah, yeah, just been sitting a long time. It's my job, I should be more used to it." He smiled once more and launched himself toward the house. He'd been here a few times before, but was suddenly perplexed: there were 2 bathrooms, right? One large one, one smaller one off Greg and Mo's bedroom... The glass patio door hissed on it's rails and the air conditioning pulled at Charlie's body. He stood in the dim living room, then spied a sliver of light to the left, through the kitchen, and remembered the bathroom was there, a few feet down the hall from the refrigerator. Someone threw on an overhead light and he winced: "Sup Charlie, just hanging in the dark?" a voice asked, and Kiko, the bartender whisked by him and opened the freezer door. "No, uh, Kiko, couldn't remember where the bathroom was."

Kiko smacked at a bag of ice in the freezer to dislodge it and yanked it out. "Right there, dude," Kiko pointed with an elbow, and moved to slip by Charlie again, stopped short, and said in a low voice: "And Charlie? That Beth girl is mostly dyke. Like, 95% or something. Just so you know."

Charlie felt the ice move away from where Kiko had held it near Charlie's leg.

He sat in the bathroom, pants down, staring at his knees and rubbing his hands together. Fuck that guy, Kiko, what does he know. She probably wouldn't blow him at the bar or something so now she's a dyke. And what the hell do I care anyway? I'm busy, got no time for women and stuff like that. Oh hell, I'm drunk and my hands hurt and I shouldn't have come here, they're probably talking about me now, whispering to her, like Kiko did to me: hey, Beth, that Charlie guy? He's all fucked up, his fiance had some kind of seizure and died on their kitchen floor, right before they were supposed to get married, now he's like a hermit or something, you could see he was weird—yeah, he seemed a little strange, she would say, and then he would come out of the bathroom and they would all put on their fake smiles and wish he would just go home so they could talk about how weird he was, like it was one of those TV shows where they trap normal people with a crazy one and make them live in an apartment with no windows. Is there a show like that? God, I haven't watched TV in so long, Emily liked those reality shows, she would laugh and try to get me to watch and of course I'd say "hell no," those people are just faking, it's garbage meant to rot your mind and make you more pliable so they can sell you window cleaner and Big Macs and deodorant and cars, they want to make sure that everyone watching these shows ends up as stupid as the people they put on them. And she would say, Oh Charlie, relax, maybe you should watch so you know what the enemy is up to? And anyway, what's wrong with deodorant, you wear deodorant.... yes, I wear deodorant. Yes, I eat frozen pizza. Yes, I drive a gasoline-engine vehicle and pay my phone bill and pay taxes, and no, I don't go to the big bank downtown and stand in the lobby beneath the domed ceiling, the stained glass, the masonic symbols pressed in gold, and take down my pants and shit on the green and white marble tile, though you can't imagine how much I really want to. No, she's right, that would solve nothing, but it would feel so wonderful, because I get shit on every day. Who shits on you Charlie? You're a college student, you wait tables—it's the whole structure, don't you see? This whole power-structure I was born into, that you were born into: like, every time a guy stares at your chest, doesn't that piss you off? Well sure, but he's not shitting on me. He is! He's shitting on you and every other woman, making you an object of his desire and nothing more. You don't think I'm desirable, then? No, no, of course I do, but—oh no, I'm talking, I'm talking out loud to my dead fiance, I'm pretty sure that's exactly what I'm doing, sitting on the toilet in my friend's house, having an argument with my fiance, who is actually not my fiance anymore and has probably rotted to bones and hair by now. That's exactly what I mean, though. Why am I talking to a dead person? Why can't I just package all the pain and fear into a capsule and slip it into someone's double mocha-chino when they aren't looking? Why can't I buy some detergent that will help scour away the need for me to talk to people who aren't here, to hide in my house and read a random pile of books because I can't fucking figure out what else to do with the rest of my life? He felt something warm on his lip and then his hand, and saw blood and knew that he had chewed through his lower lip again. As he wadded some toilet paper to hold to his lip, someone tried the doorknob, then banged on the door: "Hey, I gotta go!" they said. "Use the other one," Charlie tried to yell back, but the words came out in a whisper. He looked out the small window at the hedge and the street beyond, stood, pulled up his pants, and lifted the window screen by the corners. The space was just large enough for Charlie to wriggle through, and he ended up doing a headstand in the dirt then flipping over onto his back in the lawn. No one was there, the yard was empty, the cars all sleeping, so Charlie walked softly to his truck, climbed in, and drove home.

Charlie woke the next morning in his bed for the first time in nearly eight months. He had pulled all the bedding off and then apparently covered himself with a pile of shirts from the closet. His hand hurt, his lip hurt, and his head felt like the top had been pried off and someone had poured a mixture of sewage and seltzer water into his skull. And the phone, as phones are wont to do, was ringing. It rang for a bit, then stopped, then started again. Charlie tipped himself out of the bed and staggered to the kitchen. "Hi Mom," Charlie said, as a burp slipped up his throat into the phone. "'Scuse me," he added.

"Well hello, my healthy boy! Did you eat already? Did you forget about brunch?" she asked. Ah shit, he whispered to himself, holding the phone away from his mouth: brunch. He'd blocked it from his mind even before inflicting himself with a raging hangover. Brunch with his mother either meant lots of crying or another life-altering decision. Maybe she was going to join the Rosicrucians.

"No, no, I didn't forget, I'll be there at eleven-thirty."

"Ok my dear, will you stop and get some orange juice? The kind with extra pulp."

"Yes mom."

"I'm so excited for you to meet Roy!" she continued. "You'll like him, he was friends with your father." Huh? Charlie already felt sick and confused, who the hell was Roy?

"Who's Roy again?"

"Oh I thought I told you, he's an old friend from Pittsburgh who's visiting, he's thinking of moving out here. Didn't I tell you he'd be joining us?"

"No, I don't remember you saying anything about any Roy. He wants to move here? Why would anyone want to move to Pearson?"

"He's retiring, he likes to hunt, he—you'll like him, I'm sure. Don't forget the juice!" his mother added giddily.

"Juice, right, ok."

"Love you."

"Love you too, Mom."

Roy, Roy... Had she mentioned him and he just forgot? Oh well, what the hell. Charlie stood in the kitchen, dazed, wobbling slightly, trying to figure out when he needed to leave: the clock said 9:45, his Mom's house fifteen minutes away—then broke off his fumbling arithmetic and bolted for the bathroom, where he vomited tart liquid until his retching at last produced nothing. Brunch. Roy. Juice. He put his head against the cold side of the toilet and felt a darkness pass through his head like the shadow of a cloud.

By the time he managed to clean up and get down the stairs to the outside, the temperature had shot up into the nineties, according to the thermometer mounted next to the front door. Charlie braced himself and yanked the door open and felt heat wash over him, through him, and he slammed the door and began retching again in the hallway. His stomach settled, and he tried again, thrusting himself out into the gelatinous heat, wading over to his truck, the whole time feeling his stomach thrum more loudly than his heart had ever done. The noise of the air conditioning was comforting, even though it merely pushed the heat around for most of the drive to the grocery store. He managed the dash into the store better, then lingered in the refrigerated section for as long as he dared, fingering and replacing half a dozed different pints of ice cream before noticing a round-faced stock clerk eyeing him suspiciously. He paid for the juice—with added pulp—and made it to the truck, which, he was glad to note, chilled much more quickly this time. He knew his mother would not turn on the air unless she absolutely had to, and even now, with the temperature in the mid-nineties, would only turn it on "a smidge," so the climate in her house would be mealy, and smell of burnt food, so he chugged half a bottle of Pepto-Bismol as he drove lazily toward her house.

A black Cherokee sat in the driveway beside his mother's Subaru, and Charlie suddenly wondered if she and Roy had had sex, if Roy was the newest man in her life. It had only been a few days since Grady left, hadn't it? And why should the position of the cars make him think they had fucked. I guess I'll know soon enough, he thought. Maybe she's getting married, maybe that's this month's life-altering event. He inhaled deeply, flung himself out of the truck, and was at the front stoop, about to knock, when the wooden door opened and his mother grinned, propping open the screen door to let him by. "Charlie baby!" she said, and waited for him to turn around in the vestibule and hug her. Her long gray hair sat in two braids on either shoulder, and she wore a brilliantly patterned brown and orange sundress. Her eyes were dark and large and tear-shaped, and she was, Charlie noticed faithfully, still sharply beautiful.

"Please don't call me Charlie baby," he answered, breaking off the hug.

"Oh I know, I know, I'm just teasing you because I know you hate it so. I'll stop," she said, taking the bottle of juice and whisking him toward the living room. "Come on, come meet Roy!"

Roy sat in a corner of the couch, his legs stretched out to one side of the heavy oaken coffee table. His legs were very long, everything about him was very long: his fingers, folded into the crooks of his elbows after putting down the newspaper; his nose, long down his face and then long outward at the end; his torso, which leaned against the couch instead of bending into it, like a piece of lumber lain against a wall; even his eyes were long, and they drooped at the outside, giving his face a look of melancholic resignation. His hair was just about the only thing about him that was not long, short grey spikes at the top, shorter on the sides, a military cut. "Hiya Charlie," he said, and extended a long hand on a long arm for Charlie to shake. "Hi Roy," Charlie answered, they both sat, his mother having slipped away into the kitchen.

"Heard a lot about you, from your Ma," Roy said, tilting his head slightly to the left.

"Yeah, good," Charlie replied. "Can't say as I've heard much about you, sorry."

Roy smiled. "Nothing to be sorry about, I came up sudden, really, ain't seen Miriam in years, probably fifteen or more. Just called her up out of the blue last week, I been looking around here for a place to get out of the city."

"Well, this is pretty far out of the city, but it's kind of a city itself."

"Yeah, but fifteen minutes anyway and I can be looking for deer or walleye. Been looking up near Ralstonville, there's some pretty land up there."

"It is pretty, yup." They sat quietly for a while, listening to Miriam rattle around the kitchen, swearing lightly to herself.

"You hunt any?" Roy asked after a time.

"Me? No, never went. Not much for guns, really," Charlie said, and remembered the slapping sound of the ice cream man's pistol, the crack as the bullet hit the house where his head had just been.

"Oh," Roy said. "Fish, then?"

"Not really."

"Oh." Roy looked down at his fingernails. "Well, your Pa loved fishing, hunting too. But he wasn't around much to show you, I guess."

"Nope, not really," Charlie replied, and felt himself starting to sweat. Who the hell was this guy? Was he really trying to be his new Daddy? Weren't they both a little old to be doing an after-school special?

"Ok boys, come and get it!" his mother called, and both men, sighing with relief, filed into the dining room.

How she'd managed to burn sliced cantaloupe was the first topic of conversation, though the rest of the spread, Charlie had to admit, was awfully damn good.

"The plate was sitting by the burner, and the cantaloupe was sitting on paper towels on the plate, and the corner caught fire. I washed them off, but yes there are still burnt pieces, just eat around them!"

Both men chuckled, and filled their plates.

"So, Mom, you said you and Roy were old friends?" Charlie asked after everyone had eaten a good bit and started to settle into their seats.

"Yes, yes, for a long time, since way before you were born," she answered.

"I was there, truth be told, out in the waiting room," Roy added, and Miriam nodded assent.

"Yes you were. You tell the story, Roy."

"Ok, well, I was raised up with your Pa, you know where he was from?"

Charlie shook his head no.

"Well, up near Buckhannon, West Virginia, little town near there that ain't there now, tiny little place that you learned to mine coal in or to get the hell out of, and me and your father we got the hell out, went to the big city, and Pittsburgh seemed like a good choice so that was the city. We got there we had a '64 Chevy, two changes of clothes, and thirty-six dollars, and we met your Ma here right off, probably about two days after we dragged into town."

"When was this?" Charlie interrupted. His Mom and Roy glanced at each other.

"1980?" Miriam said.

"'81, I think," Roy answered.

"Charlie was born September 29th, 1982, so yes, maybe it was 1981, early spring."

"Ha, I think Scott had a damn dashiki in the trunk, thought he would be stylish." With the invocation of Charlie's father's name, they all fell silent and turned inward for a moment.

"Yes, he was a crazy bastard," Roy said.

"He was a bastard, fer sure," Miriam answered, adding a Valley Girl sneer to the end of her curse.

"So what happened?" Charlie asked. He had never cared to know more about his father until this moment, and he wondered if the hangover had anything to do it, the same way hangovers can make you feel especially horny.

"So," Roy went on, "we drove on up to Pittsburgh and were staying in a hotel, eight dollars a night and fleas everywhere, and went looking for jobs and both found one the same day, and to celebrate we went to a bar to hear some music, and boy they were playing some godawful noise but Scott liked it, there were folks with green hair and ripped up clothes and there was your mother, half her hair shaved off and a ring in her nose," Roy laughed quietly, and Miriam's hand went up to smooth the hair on the top of her head.

"You were into punk? I always thought you were a hippie, Mom."

"I was into getting away, away, away from my father, and that was where you went in those days if you wanted to get away. And so I did, and there was Scott, and he swept me off my feet."

"Yes, we both tried," Roy said, "but Scott was a charmer, boy. We all shared a place for a minute, and your mother tried real hard to cook, and then—what, you went to school and Scott got a job working for the city?"

"That's right, and you started up with that girl, what was her name, the one who looked like a ostrich and dressed like a vampire—"

"Carly, well, I hadn't thought about her in a long time. She was more'n a little crazy, that one."

"So you guys all lived together? That's wild," Charlie said.

"Yes, for a few months, anyway," Miriam replied, and started clearing away plates.

"Oh let me help you," Roy said, and rose to help her.

"No, I got it. More coffee?" both men answered yes, and Miriam disappeared into the kitchen.

"Tell you what," Roy said as the door swung behind her, "your Mom is a much better cook these days."

Charlie laughed. "No doubt, in, like, the last three or four years she figured out something, it's actually edible."

"She damn near poisoned all three of us once trying to make some Lebanese thing with lamb in it, I recall. Your Pa did most of the cooking when she was in school, or so he said. I never knew he could cook, whole time we was growing up."

"Do you ever hear from him?" Roy's face darkened, and his head tilted again.

"Well, I didn't—not much, and—she didn't tell you?"

"Tell me what?"

Roy sighed and began picking at the corner of a napkin. "He passed on about eight months ago, stomach cancer, down in Houston." Charlie felt the walls wobble and the temperature in the room shoot up and he grabbed the sides of his chair, afraid he might float up into the sky.

"Well, shit."

"Sorry, man, I thought she'd a told you. I really did."

"Nope," Charlie shook his head. They were both silent for a while.

"Ok, then, let me tell you how your Dad and I left for the city, the real story," Roy said, just as Miriam pushed through the saloon doors with a pot of coffee. "Here you go," she said, and poured them both a cup. Charlie stared at her, watched her pour; her body seemed entirely flat, two-dimensional. "Well," she said, and noticed both men staring at her. "What's going on here? Some kind of cabal?"

"You didn't tell him about Scott?" Roy asked, voice creaky. She drew her lips up small and looked down at the surface of the table. "No, not yet, I just—Charlie, I wanted to wait for the right time."

"Uh-huh."

"Listen, why don't you go outside and look at that flower bed you want dug and figure out how much dirt we got to buy. I'm gonna talk to Charlie a minute," Roy said.

"No, I—" she stopped herself. "Yes, ok, that's a good idea." She paused at the door and turned to face Charlie. "I'm sorry, I should have told you," she said, speaking way too fast, and pushed through the door.

Roy and Charlie sat, staring at their coffee. The sound of his mother crying came through the door.

"Well then, let's see, where were we... ok, well, your Dad was a wild one, and I was along for the ride, that's how it was when we was kids. We did country stuff, we hunted and fished and blew shit up, and then we got older and started smoking, drinking, reefer, whatever. One day Charlie got himself some LSD, and now we thought we'd done LSD before, yes we took it before and we giggled and walked around campfires playing with sticks, but I don't know if we ever took real acid before, because this shit Scott got was serious. It was clear, like tiny little slides from chemistry class. I'll always remember it because we each took two of those little bastards, took'em one Saturday afternoon and blam! Nearly took our heads off, we got talking the usual crazy stuff you do when you on acid, and Scott gets this idea he wants to go see his Pa preach. Now, Scott's Pa was a holy roller—didja know that? No?—he was, a scary old man even more crazy than Scott, had a whole tribe of crazies he'd preach to, made up his own denomination and everything, even the Baptists ran the county wouldn't mess with him. So yeah, Scott gets to thinking that the acid is making us kinda, transparent, I guess invisible is what he meant but he kept saying, 'no, no, just see-through,' and he thought it would put the fear into his Pa to see us, or not see us, or see through us, during Saturday night mass," Roy paused, and took a sip of his coffee. "Damn. Yes, we went up there, scary little church full a scary people, and we went in and the whole church turned and looked at us, I swear I will never forget that till the day I die, it was like they had one head, and their eyes were fire, not red fire, the bluish-white kind. I turned around and ran, ran right off into the woods and back to the main road before I even looked back and saw Scott weren't with me." He paused again. Charlie was trying hard to take all this in, he never cared to know about his Dad until now and Jesus, this is not what he'd never pictured when he didn't think about it.

"I wandered around and eventually went home and went to sleep. Woke up next night cause your Pa was rapping on my window, he's all torn up, got cuts all up and down his body, and he's wearing someone else's clothes. 'Come on,' he says, 'we're goin." And I went, I got in that '64 Chevy and rode straight through till Pittsburgh. We stopped first and stole everything we could from his Pa's place. Well, he did, anyhow, I waited in the car. Didn't have much, anyhow, but Scott got his stuff anyhow and that thirty-six dollars."

"What the fuck," Charlie said, the words popping out like he'd been holding his breath.

"Indeed. I never did take LSD again after that, I tell you. Scott did, though, which surprised the hell out of me, cause he told me, once we got to Pittsburgh, that the whole congregation had grabbed him and his Pa had him tied up to a tree outside, naked, and then he went back to preaching, and every so often he's stop, and the whole gaggle of'em would come out and speak in tongues and hit Scott with sticks, belts, whatever they had. Went on all night, he said, then everyone went home and his Pa just left him there, tied to that tree."

Charlie realized he had dug his fingernails very deep into bottom of the chair. "I—, I don't even know. Wow."

"Yeah," Roy agreed. "Some crazy shit. But anyway, I thought he'd want me to tell you that, the story of how he got here, and met your Mom, maybe give you a little idea of what kind of man he was." The two mens' eyes met just as Miriam burst through the swinging door, sobbing.

"I should have told you! Oh I know I should have.... but I found out right when, when Emily—" she fell into a chair and blew her nose theatrically. Charlie turned his head, and saw his mother, 17 years old, running away from her strict Lebanese family straight into the arms of a an 18 year old hillbilly running away from his own orthodoxy, and he felt suddenly very calm, even strangely rested.

"No, no, it's ok, Mom. Really. I can see why, really."

"Really? I would never try to hurt you, you know that, I always—"

"Really," he interrupted, stood up, and walked purposefully to the bathroom, where he vomited for the third time that morning.

CHAPTER 5

This time, when the song tried to sneak up on Charlie, when the tinkling grew louder and closer to the window he'd propped open with an empty beer bottle, he was ready for it, he had done his homework and had a plan. The tune was "Music Box Dancer," not "Turkey in the Straw," as he'd first thought; he'd spent most of the week after he'd had his internet connection turned back on looking up small details like this one, plugging holes in his understanding of what had happened to him, and why. But these searches caused him to neglect his reading, and so he was back in his recliner, thudding his way through *Invisible Man*. The temperature had dropped sharply in the last few days, allowing Charlie to shut off the air conditioning for the first time in almost three months. Big changes were afoot, it seemed, and he went through his evenings in a state of heightened expectation. Perhaps, he said to himself as the ice cream truck's song wheezed at the curb in front of his house, this is what I've been waiting for.

He drew back the curtain softly and peeked out: yes, it was the same ice cream truck, a white bread box covered with stickers, the closed service window facing Charlie's lawn. The driver had parked, and dusk had passed, it was fully night. The song played on. So this is it, what do I do? Charlie put his book on the table and rubbed the side of his head. Last time I was nice, and he shot a gun at me, so that won't work, and I'm sick of being nice anyway. He stood and started to pace, clicking his fingers together like pincers as he did. His stomach was balled tightly and his throat was dry. His bowels began to rumble, and he headed to the bathroom for the fifth time in the last six hours: he had dropped the frozen pizza from his diet and instead was eating mostly fruits and yogurt and whole grains, and his body was taking its time catching up. He couldn't believe there was actually that much waste in his body, that he could shit five times in a six hour span, but there it was—and there it was, his course of action spelled out for him in the knotty coils at the bottom of the toilet bowl. He went to the kitchen and got a large plastic serving spoon—after first rejecting the slotted variety—and a Tupperware bowl, then returned to the bathroom and scooped as much of his shit into the bowl as he could without puking. On his way out the door, he grabbed an empty glass bottle, and thus encumbered, bottle in his right hand, serving spoon and bowl full of shit in his left, he crept down the stairs and out the door and toward the street, following the path worn in the grass. When he was ten feet or so from the back of the truck, he stopped, gauged the distance, and flung the bottle up over the truck so it landed and shattered on the other side, near the driver. The sound of the bottle breaking acted on him like a starter's pistol, and in one motion, he dashed toward the passenger's side of the truck, shifted the spoon to his right hand, and scooped out a healthy portion of turd, which he then catapulted through the open window of the truck, eliciting a howl from its occupant. Charlie squealed in triumph and quickly flung another scoop, heard another howl, spun on his heels, and ran back around the corner of the house, dropping the tools of his assault in the lawn. He stopped around the corner and breathed heavily, his hands on his knees. Someone in the street was screaming and banging on the side of the truck, and Charlie smiled and sneaked quietly back up the stairs to settle in and watch the show.

The man in the street was the same one who'd shot at Charlie a few weeks earlier, there was no doubt about it, and a lucky thing too, as it dawned on him that he could have hit a perfect stranger with spoonfuls of shit, instead of Big Chief Cavuto. Charlie sat on the floor and squinted through the space beneath the curtain as the man let loose a torrent of obscenity and waved his pistol in the air like a flag. His white muscle shirt was speckled with brown, as was, to Charlies' delight, the side of his face.

"I know you're in there! I know where you live, you dumb cocksucker! Come out you fucking pussy! Pussy shitdog motherfucker come out here and I will shoot your fucking ass!" He pointed the pistol at the window and Charlie ducked down instinctively, but no shot came. He risked another peek and saw that the man had disappeared. The horns blaring "Music Box Dancer" stopped, and the street was quiet and curved beneath the streetlights, a diorama trapped beneath a glass bell. The man emerged again from behind the truck, wiping his face with a towel. He stopped wiping and stared at the window Charlie hid behind, stared into Charlie's eyes, it seemed, but Charlie was not afraid, not even as the man raised his arm and pointed his finger like a gun directly at Charlie's head. "You're gonna wish you were dead, friend," he yelled, and made the hammer of his finger-pistol fire an imaginary shot. Sirens sounded somewhere, and Charlie turned and sat with his back against the wall, facing the scene of his recent hermitage: the enormous bookshelf, the piles of books on the floor beside the recliner, the scabbed quarter-sawn planks of the floor, the mottled yellow wallpaper... a curious energy gathered at the base of his spine, a crackling ball of electricity, and his mouth was filled with the taste of metal. Ha! I don't wish I was dead, in fact, I'm finally alive! He turned and looked out the window once more and saw the man leaning against his truck, smoking a cigarette, staring up at Charlie. Stare away, fool! The police will be here soon and what will you say? A ghost threw shit at you? You didn't see me, no one saw me, and you have a gun and I'm sure you don't have a license for it. I win. You lose. Have a bomb pop and lick your wounds—oh wait, no, don't, they have my shit all over them.

The sirens grew louder and then slowed to a stop as the police car pulled to the curb. Charlie watched as the same two policemen who'd come when the ice cream man shot at him walked slowly to where the shit-spattered goon was standing. He couldn't make out what they were saying, but Cavuto was gesturing wildly, pointing up at Charlie's window, recreating the scene. After several minutes of ranting and gesticulating, he stopped and crossed his arms, and one of the policemen drifted down the path toward Charlie's door, out of his line of sight. He crawled across the living room floor, standing only when he reached the linoleum floor of the kitchen, and waited for the doorbell to ring. It rang as soon he put his hand on the doorknob and he started, then pulled the door open and went down to talk with the police.

The main door at the bottom of the stairs was open—had he forgotten to pull it closed?—and the shorter of the two cops stood on the other side of the threshold, looking up through the screen door. He cocked his head like a dog as Charlie reached the landing, grinning despite himself. "Ah, yeah, it is you," he said.

"Hello," Charlie answered, "can I help you?" He noticed that the policeman had shaved his mustache.

"Are you—" the cop looked down the notepad he held in his hand for a long time.

"Charlie Price, this is my house, yes, what can I do for you? Is there some trouble outside? I heard a man yelling." The cop cocked his head at Charlie again and sighed.

"Are you totally fucked in the head? I mean, are you, maybe, suicidal?"

"Are you asking me in your professional capacity, officer—" Charlie leaned over and looked at his badge, "Jenks?"

Jenks paused again for long time, staring at Charlie. "Ok, we'll try it that way. Mr. Price, have you heard or seen anything out of the ordinary outside your apartment in the last few hours?"

"Well, yes," Charlie said, "I told you, I heard a man screaming and cursing."

"Uh-huh. And you have no idea why he was screaming?"

"No sir, I was reading and he started in cursing and such, so I looked out the window and he was screaming in the street. He looked pretty mad."

"He was pretty mad, in fact. It seems someone hit him with a ball of wet shit." Charlie burped a giggle, and put his hand in front of his mouth.

"Wow, that's too bad. Why would they do that?" He knew he was still grinning like a dolphin, but he couldn't help himself.

"I don't know," the cop answered. "Why don't you come out and ask him?"

"Oh no, no no no," Charlie said, "That guy shot at me, I'm not talking to him."

"He shot at you, huh?"

"Oh come on, you came after he shot at me, when I called you guys."

"So this guy shot at you, and yet you have no idea why someone would hit him with shit?"

Charlie was not grinning anymore. He could feel sweat creeping down the back of his neck.

"No idea," he said.

"So, how about you come down to the station with us and maybe we can figure it out?"

"Why?"

"Why? Maybe you can help us. Did you see anybody sneaking around here?" Jenks crossed his hands in front of his belt, the notepad beneath them.

"Well, um, now that you mention it, yeah, there was this guy with dreadlocks and lots of tattoos hanging out on the sidewalk earlier. He was, ah, talking on a cell phone, I think, that's what it looked like."

Jenks stared hard at a place just above Charlie's eyebrows.

"Ok, great, so why don't you come down to the station and look at some pictures and maybe you can spot the guy for us. Or, you can wait here with the guy who got hit with shit, I'm pretty sure he's going to hang around and look for the guy himself, even though he said he would leave."

Charlie rubbed the side of his head and thought for a minute.

"Yes, very well, I will help you gentleman with your enquiries. I would like to be sure that the man who shot at me is gone before I leave the house, though, please. Ok?" Jenks sighed again.

"Ok, just come on out when he drives away," he said, "and don't lock yourself in up there, it will piss me off like you wouldn't believe."

"No sir, officer," Charlie said, and the grin slithered back into his face.

The police station was much quieter—and smaller—than Charlie thought it would be. Jenks and Rouse, the taller of the two, had driven Charlie silently through downtown; neither spoke until they pulled up to the curb across from the station, where Rouse commanded Charlie to "get out," which he did, and "come on," which he also did, and finally "sit there and wait," in a crooked chair in the main hallway. And Charlie waited, looking at his fingernails, at the bulletin board scattered with grainy photos and drawings and fliers offering cars, guns, and a boat for sale, at the empty water cooler at the end of the hall, at the linoleum floor worn shiny everywhere but at the edges, black with dirt. The door Jenks and Rouse had gone through was closed, as were most of the doors on the hall, and everything was quiet.

Charlie's eyelids started to droop. He shook his head and looked around the hall again, then heard a radio suddenly blare from one of the rooms near the water cooler. He stood and shook his hands, bent over and touched his toes, and stood up again to see Jenks watching him through the doorway. He smiled, and Jenks shook his head. "Ok kid, get in here," he said, and gestured for Charlie to walk past him.

The door closed behind Charlie. Rouse was nowhere to be seen. He looked over his shoulder and saw that Jenks had vanished as well. There was a desk in the middle of the room, and the man behind the desk was immense, with a gut that seemed tired of protruding and a head the shape of a cement block, but significantly larger. His hair was grey and swept back from his forehead, and his eyes and nose were tiny, which was disconcerting given the size of his head and his very wide, very red mouth. Charlie could not stop staring at him. The man, in turn, stared at the same spot above Charlie's eyebrows that Jenks had, and Charlie wondered if he had some dirt—or maybe shit?—there, and he licked his fingers and rubbed at his head jerkily.

"Why am I looking at you?" the man said, as though continuing a conversation begun twenty minutes ago.

"Uh, hi, well, uh, the two cops, I mean, the two police guys there told me to come look at some pictures. Yes, that's why I came with them, yes. But I don't know who you are, sorry."

"Shinevsky. Detective Shinevsky." He looked down and rustled through the sprawl on the surface of his desk, found a wooden nameplate, and turned it so that the letters now faced Charlie. It read "Shinevsky."

"If I ever find out who keeps doing that..." he muttered, and went back to staring at Charlie's eyebrows. "And you are Charlie Price, resident of 261 Bundy Ave, and these, I believe, are yours." He reached down behind his desk and brought out Charlie's Tupperware bowl and serving spoon.

"Ah, no, don't think those are mine. I mean, I have ones like that, I think. Am I here to make a cake?"

"Listen to me, you ignorant little boy," Shinevsky said, voice growing taut, "what you did would be considered lewd and lascivious, and could be classified as assault, no matter who you did it to. I'll admit, it's a pretty creative bit of perversion, but the fact that you chose to do it to the man you chose to do it to made your decision much more foolish than you can possibly imagine."

Charlie shifted in his chair and looked down at the ground, then felt the metal in the base of his spine get hot, and stared back at Shinevsky. "He shot a gun at me and you guys did nothing. Shot a gun! He could have killed me. Why is he not arrested?"

Shinevsky slumped a bit. "We're working on it."

"Working on it?"

"Yes, working on it, and the officers who told you to stay away from that man were trying to keep you out of trouble, out of a potentially dangerous situation. You really don't know what you are fucking with here, son."

"I'm not your son," Charlie sneered.

"No you're not. You're the son of Miriam Price, who is a friend of mine, and if she wasn't, you'd be in a holding cell with the rest of the undesirables. You are a college student—"

"Was a college student—"

"Right," he continued, "you were a college student, then your girlfriend killed herself, and you dropped out. Now you work at Top Gun Security, and like so many other ignorant, over-educated young people, spend your precious life doing fuck all. So. Once again. Why did you hit Derek Cavuto with shit?"

Charlie stood up fast, too fast, and his chair thunked on the floor behind him. "She was my fiance, and she did not commit suicide, she had an aneurysm. And what I do with my time is really not your concern. And—if I were to hit someone with shit, which is pretty weird, I would probably hit a fucking psycho ice-cream man who tried to shoot me because I asked him to turn the goddamn turkey in the straw song off!" He spun around and righted the chair, then threw himself down in it and did his best to look bad-ass.

Now Shinevsky was looking him in the eye. "I thought it was 'Music Box Dancer'."

"Some trucks play that one, he plays 'Turkey In The Straw'. No, you're right, it is 'Music Box Dancer'. But what, who cares?" Shinevsky nodded, picked up a pen, and scribbled something on his desk blotter.

"Ok, regardless, you are in deep shit now, no pun intended, and there isn't a lot I can do to help you, except tell you to get out of town for a while. Maybe for a long while."

"How do you know my Mom?"

"That—" he sighed. "I met Miriam soon after she and your Dad got here from, where was it?"

"Pittsburgh."

"Right, Pittsburgh. And you were there too. So, I've known her a long time, and I haven't told her yet what you've got yourself involved in, but I'm going to have to, because she might be at risk now too."

"What? What are you—why are you fucking with me? The guy shot at me, stood in the middle of the street and shot at me."

"I understand that, but I am not fucking with you, I am telling you that there will be much less of a chance somebody does something to Miriam if you got the hell out of town and let me try and placate these bastards while I try to figure out how to get them all in prison. Put Cavuto in jail for shooting at you, for discharging a weapon in city limits, he'll be out in three weeks, and then you and your Mom are well and truly fucked. In the meantime, you get out of town, and stop throwing shit at people, you twisted little fucker." Shinevsky sat back and crossed his fingers over his belly. He'd been performing this move a lot lately, because he was convinced he was going to die soon, largely due to a recurring nightmare where he carried a lit torch through a swamp, muck up to his chest, till he reached an old cannon, which then fizzled when he tried to light it. Crossing his fingers over his belly made him feel safer, somehow, and the nightmares did go away, but he would die soon, little more than a year from now, falling asleep at the wheel of his car on the way home from the late shift.

"Thanks for the advice, I'll take it under consideration. Can I go?" Charlie asked.

Shinevsky moved his head slowly from side to side. "Stupid little boy. Go on, and try thinking about your Mother a little bit, instead of just fucking around and worrying about yourself."

"Nice," Charlie said, and turned and walked out of the room. Once in the hall, he couldn't remember which way was out, and the walls seemed much closer together than before. He looked up, and saw the tops of the walls beginning to curl inward. He shook his head, and turned to see the door open and Jenks come through, carrying a Styrofoam cup. "Figure it out?" he said.

"Yeah, thanks," Charlie answered, and walked past Jenks, out the door, and into a dank morning light. The metallic feeling in his spine shuddered upward and outward, down along his thighs, up into his rib cage, his shoulders. It felt like another skeleton was growing atop the old one, and it felt fucking fantastic.

CHAPTER 6

Charlie didn't bother to phone Big Al when Little Al, or Al the younger, or Big Al's concubine (as Charlie thought of him when he was particularly annoyed), was late for work, since he was always late because of Big Al, and Big Al always dropped him off, so really there was no point. And so, the Monday morning after his second adventure with the police, Charlie sat waiting for Little Al to float through the door of the trailer, smirking, as was his habit, or his nature, Charlie had never bothered to figure out which. He stared vaguely upwards, at the far upper left-hand corner where two walls joined the ceiling, where a patch of grey mold had formed. The patch looked like many things, Charlie found he could stare at it and make out various shapes, resemblances, a bit like looking at clouds, or at the white noise on the television. If he stared long and hard, and tried not to blink, the patch would seem to shimmy, and even start to radiate different colors. He tried not to stare long and hard very often, though he felt a strong compulsion to do so.

The hollow thunk of the Hummer's door closing shook Charlie from his speculations, and he checked the clock to see how late little Al was this time. In fact, he was early, which was unusual enough to set Charlie on edge, given the events of the previous evening and the small, angry hours of sleep he'd managed to grab since then. The Als were never early, neither of them were ever anything but late and obnoxious. Charlie peeked through the tiny window set in the door of the trailer and saw big Al stepping heavily down from the Hummer's cab. What's this? Did little Al finally find a better sugar daddy? Charlie turned and went back to the desk and pretended to leaf through a copy of *Guns and Ammo*. He was checking out a particularly sexy Mauser when the door final creaked open. Big Al looked in, met Charlie's eyes, and looked away, muttering "hello" in his general direction.

"What's up Al? To what do I owe the pleasure?" Charlie asked, laying the magazine on the desk.

"Yeah, Charlie. It's about time, you think?" Al was looking around the trailer, rubbing his hands together. "Yeah, about time for a new trailer, I think."

"Why, what's wrong with this one?"

Al turned and stared at Charlie suddenly. His face was dark and sagging, his eyes bloodshot. Charlie leaned forward, suddenly worried.

"Look, how long you been workin' here, Charlie?"

"Six months, almost seven."

"I think it's time you moved on, did something better, you don't need this shit, I mean—" he paused and rubbed hard at the end of his nose, "come on, you got a college degree, you could be doing something better with your life. Dontcha think?"

"I don't have a degree, I'm three classes short," Charlie replied, tilting his head so that it was nearly parallel with the desk top.

"Whatever!" Al yelled suddenly. "You're done! I'm tryin' to be nice here, I'll give you a month salary, here—" he dug a wad of bills out of his pocket and threw them on the table. "You're done. Take whatever shit is yours, leave the keys, and get out."

"What—wha—why? What did I do"

"Ella says you been spying on her." His voice was suddenly flat, like he was repeating lines he'd rehearsed far too often.

"Ella? The aromatherapy lady?"

"Ella says you been spying, I told her I would get rid of you if she didn't call the cops. Now get the fuck out, you're fired."

"Wow, what a lot of bullshit. Ok!" Charlie felt a sudden unfolding of energy in his stomach, it made the metal in his bones sing out. He pocketed the wad of cash and stomped past Al to the door. "You poor sad old fairy," he said, without turning to look at his former boss, and thrust himself out into the sunlight. It was hot today, but Charlie felt strong, so strong that the heat fell off him in ripples. He thought he saw Little Al's head peeking over the top of the Hummer's dashboard, but he didn't bother looking too hard. Big

Al was right: it was time to move on. He could take a week or two and do nothing but read, plow through all the rest of the books on the shelves, then pack up what he needed and go, somewhere, out into the world, Alaska maybe, or Cheyenne, Wyoming. He always liked the sound of Cheyenne, Wyoming, it sounded big and wild and full of air. Hell yeah! I'll start right now, he thought, grab some beer on the way home, make a party of it, stay up and read for days and not go to sleep... I need a cell phone, too, I need to get back in touch. He slammed the door of his pickup and pulled out of the lot, humming to himself, oscillating, watching the road spread itself out in front of his wheels, imagining all the other roads it connected to, the way road leads on to road, like the man said.

And plow through books he did, for the next twenty hours, reading faster than he ever had, and with total immersion. Only when he realized he was about to piss his pants did he set *Invisible Man* aside, and he had finished it and *The Erector Set* and *The Little Book of Fishing* and *King Rat* and was a third of the way through *The Grapes of Wrath* before he noticed night had come and gone, and that he hadn't eaten since the previous day. He stuffed his mouth with cold tabbouleh and then tried, reluctantly, to sleep. His head spun and wobbled and the metal in his bones kept vibrating, but he found he could modulate the vibrations, tune them to a lower frequency that was actually quite soothing. The metal in my bones. How long have I been thinking that? How long have I been taking for granted the idea that I have some kind of iron frame growing inside my body? This is bad. He opened his eyes and looked at the darkened window. It's night again. I must have slept all day, I slept hard, I remember nothing, not even getting in bed. Metal in my body. I must be losing it, this is the psychotic break, I'm snapping and they'll find me gibbering in some gutter and put me in the state hospital and fill me with drugs and electricity. But shit, no, it feels good, it feels wonderful, I know there's not really metal growing in my body, it just feels that way, it's a metaphor. Just repeat that, Charlie, say it every time you wake up: it's just a metaphor. And it's not a metaphor for me going crazy, it's a metaphor for me, finally, getting better.

He swung his feet over the edge of the bed and looked at them. They looked like feet, like his feet, perfectly normal, typically ugly, in need of some serious nail clipping. As he stood and started toward the kitchen, he heard a banging noise, very close, and he jumped: someone was knocking on his door, not the downstairs door, but his apartment door. He stared at the door, and the banging began again, this time accompanied by a thickly-accented, worried-sounding voice "Charlie? Charlie are you at home?" Ah, the landlord. Patel whatisname. I really should learn his first name, I sound ignorant. To myself. To—whatever. "Yeah, just a second." He checked his clothes quickly for rude stains and went to open the door. "Hi Mr. Patel."

Mr. Patel looked at Charlie like he was trying to remember where his keys were, eyes slightly unfocused and pointed in the general area of Charlie's face. All at once he snapped back into focus.

"Yes, hello Charlie."

"Um. Well, what can I do for you?"

"You should be coming downstairs with me now, I think," Mr. Patel answered.

"Sure, ok, ok..." Charlie followed Mr. Patel down the stairs. As they descended, Charlie saw that it wasn't night quite yet, but that the last, malty hour before dusk hung in the air. Mr. Patel went out the front door without stopping or looking back, and Charlie went after him. He had to hurry to keep up through the parking lot, out to the far corner by the dumpster where Charlie parked his truck. Mr. Patel stopped in front of the truck, folded his arms, and stared at Charlie, his face twitching slightly. The pickup was trashed, every window reduced to a jagged gape, tires slashed, headlights pried off so they hung loose or sat on the pavement. "Later, chief" and "cocksucker" were spray painted in black and red on the side facing Charlie and Mr. Patel. And it smelled awful, awful in a way Charlie could not place, until he peered in the broken driver's side window and saw the dead dog, guts spread out on the dashboard and hanging off the steering wheel like fishing nets set out to dry. Charlie retched and nearly vomited, caught his nose in his hand, swallowed hard, and stepped away. "Holy shit," he said, and continued staring at the truck. He couldn't look away.

"Yes, exactly, holy shit. This is very bad indeed, Charlie," Mr. Patel said after a while.

"Yeah, very bad. My truck! I—I don't know who would do this, Mr. Patel! Why did they do this? Jesus..." He turned and felt his hands curling into fists, his spine hardening into a spear; he was not shocked to discover he was getting an erection, but he was a little puzzled by the fact that he was not shocked.

"I think we have a problem, Charlie."

"You got that right. Whose dog is it?"

"That is my dog," Mr. Patel said, and Charlie saw that he was crying, and that he was straining very hard not let more tears escape. Mr. Patel had great difficulty restraining his emotions and devoted a lot of time to practicing this restraint; so much time, in fact, that his wife had left him two years earlier and taken their sons back to Toronto, and it was shortly thereafter that the dog, who he called "Dog," being unused to having pets of any kind, had showed up in his yard, clearly starving. Dog had been his best friend since then, and as he tried to keep his tears in, he wondered if he had loved Dog even more than his wife, or his children, or even his parents.

"Oh, wow. I'm so sorry, Mr. Patel. I don't understand it, what happened."

"What happened has happened," Mr. Patel answered, suddenly brusque; "and what must happen now is you must find some new place to live. Very soon. Tomorrow." He turned and walked back across the parking lot to his Audi, opened the drawer, and took out a large envelope. "It is legal, I have the right to tell you to move if I feel you are dangerous, or that something dangerous could happen because of you." His voice grew softer. "I like you Charlie, I never have any trouble from you, well, no, I have had some trouble but I think you are a good boy, and the trouble is not your causing. I will give you back your month's rent and your security deposit." He handed Charlie a smaller envelope he'd withdrawn from the larger one."And please, now, go pack your things, you must go. I know you do not have many things, but the larger things I can have sent to you where you find a place to live, or I can put them in storage, I own the storage facility at Meeker Hill and—"

"No, no, no, that's fine, I'll take care of it," Charlie interrupted him, and sat down in a heap on the pavement. "I'll pack what I need and you can just, oh who the fuck cares, just sell it, there's nothing worth anything up there." He sat and held the envelope by a corner and stared at the dark grey patch between his crossed legs. There were tiny bits of broken glass and pebbles and a streak of rubber there, and it looked like the evening sky. Charlie felt a hand on his head, and heard Mr. Patel say "Good luck" very softly, then heard the thunk of his car door, the car starting and grinding away, and then quiet. He sat and stared at the pavement and let his mind uncoil, words and images and urges and sounds all fluttering by, grit floating in solution, none of it sticking to him or to the other bits of flotsam, every piece drifting away from every other. Gradually, some of the stray bits of cognition began to coalesce, rising from the undifferentiated field to form a single, concrete thought that played itself over and over in Charlie's mind: How did they get ahold of his dog?

This thought soon gave off echoes, new shoots, associations: and why the dog? Do they hate dogs? Or, does he hate dogs, the bastard that did this, I do know who did it, and Mr. Patel knows and if I call the fucking cops again, the fucking ice cream man will know that I called them, and if that's what he wants, well fuck yeah, bring it on, just like the President said. Don't fuck with my freedom, Mr. Softy. Charlie clambered to his feet, took one last look at his truck, and went back into his apartment to see what he had to pack.

All of his clothes fit into two small suitcases, as did a few toiletries, and he put a single fork, knife, spoon, and his favorite coffee mug (the one that said "MUG") into a canvas bag, along with some cans of soup and beans. After this initial, panicky burst of stuffing bags and cases, Charlie slowed, told himself the Gestapo was not coming to take him away, after all, and that he should be at least a little more circumspect. The situation seemed a function of cosmic order, after all. He was ready to go, to move on, more than ready, in fact, and now he was being prodded—shoved—thrown into the next phase of his life. He stood in the kitchen and took a breath, tried to inhale for as long as he could, feeling his lungs stretched, the molecules of oxygen breaking into component particles, fusing with the metal that had grown along his spine and now too along his shoulders and hips, firing a furnace in his belly and then exhaling... The kitchen, what did he need from the kitchen... He was going to be traveling, living in motels and truck stops and diners for a while, so in addition to his cutlery and cans, he needed, duh, a can opener; a melamine bowl Emily had bought at some Chinese grocery in Pittsburgh; some Tupperware that wasn't too torn up; Emily had touched all these things, her own molecules were in them but ah! All the more reason to take a few, he was getting stronger, he didn't need to avoid her presence, he needed to let it become a small, quiet, important part of him. Oh! He felt a panic once more: what if there are not enough traces of her, not enough molecules to make her pieces fuse right? He needed the metal to be an alloy, the wrong amount of anything would fuck it all up. He put the peeler that had made its way into his hand down on the table and went into the living room. The unread books were on the top shelves, the ones he'd finished on the lower ones. There were, perhaps, 25 or 30 left, maybe less; he'd read the bottom 7 shelves, there were 3 others, and each shelf held—15 books? 20? He'd never bothered to count, even when he listed all the titles and printed them out.

This is where she lives, he thought. What's the last book, I wonder? He stood on his tip toes and took down the top-left most book, fighting a voice in his head that said, "it's like reading the last page first..." It was thick and short, so he had to dig a bit to pull it loose, but at last it popped out: *Tinker Tailor Soldier Spy*, John LeCarre, wow, yeah, that was a good one, and the one beside that on the shelf was *The Honourable Schoolboy*, then *Smiley's People*, all LeCarre and Emily had found them all in different shops, they were the first ones he'd read, and then—Charlie heard an enormous click, a shifting of gears, and he started to pull the other books from the top shelf: *Beyond Good and Evil*, *Man's Search For Himself*, *Lord of the Rings*... now he was yanking them off the shelf, scanning the titles, throwing them on the ground. He'd read them all, every one, read them all already and started again—how many times? Oh fuck, this is messed up, *Foundation*, *Collected Poems of Dylan Thomas*, *The Idiot*... He stopped throwing books on the floor and grabbed the printout on the table beside the recliner. There were the titles, the little check marks beside the ones he'd finished... He flipped through the pages, found a page with incomprehensible scrawl dragging diagonally against the lines, another with a series of doodles, mostly eyeballs with hair on them, and nothing else. Had he not kept track before this? Maybe he started the record keeping because he'd already read them all and knew it, or maybe he destroyed previous journals. Maybe he'd read them all a thousand times, maybe his apartment was a place where time ceased, maybe he should stop it. Stop it. He had been not so good, now he was better, he was getting better, his bones were growing metal and electricity filled his veins so just stop it. It's just a metaphor. He didn't need the books. He pulled one at random from the bottom shelf: *Winesburg, Ohio*. Nope, hadn't read that one, *The Group*, never read that, he just got confused, got out of order, mixed up where he was supposed to start from, he hadn't read them all, Emily had picked out most of them, her molecules were in his gut and his brain, he didn't need to read them all and anyway he couldn't, he had a new path. He scanned the list: 37 titles without check marks. He could take them with him, if he wanted, but no—it was time to go.

But go where? He went to the kitchen table with a pen and a piece of paper and began to make a list:

> <u>Need to get:</u>
> Car
> Cell phone
> Map(s)
> camp stove?
> pots and pans?
> new books
> phone numbers: Mom, ?
>
> <u>Need to bring:</u>
> laptop
> clothes
> personal hygiene stuff
> food/utensils
>
> <u>Possible Destinations:</u>
> Alaska (?)
> Cheyenne, WY
> Houston, TX

Pittsburgh (far enough?)
Europe
China

China sounded far away, and Europe seemed a place of controlled adventure, but he knew he hadn't the money for either destination, at least not yet. Pittsburgh would be easy, he knew people there and could stay with them, but if he was going to fling himself into the next stage of his life, a 45 minute drive would probably not cut it. And it might still be close enough for the ice-cream man to track him down—Derek! Ha! So, Mr. Bad-ass, wife-beater with 50's haircut pistol shooting numb nuts was named Derek, of all things! He probably had a street name, "Spider," or "Slick," or something hip-hop: "T-Freeze" or something equally stupid and bovine. Derek. I'm not sure, Charlie mused, hand holding the pen aloft, that I can really and truly change my life, emerge from the cocoon, reinvent Charlie Price in some strange, new landscape knowing I was there because I ran away from a guy named Derek. If his name was Pasquale, or even Vince, maybe, but Derek? Fuck that. He looked down at his lists and added a new column at the bottom:

Need for Project D. (Complete before leaving):
Spray paint? Oil paint? Paintballs/gun?
Matches/Lighter
~~Dead animal~~
Garbage? Restaurant oil?
~~Explosives? (look on internet)~~

I really don't want to hurt anyone, he thought, looking at the last item and briefly imagining the ice cream truck exploding like trucks explode on movie screens, but with many more visible body parts flying through the air, and maybe some screaming. But no, I just want to embarrass him, humiliate him so that his life, too, changes totally, so that he has to reinvent himself as a mouse, or some other skittering, scared thing. That's all. So explosions, guns, personal injury, all those things will just make him mad or dead, not scared.

Realizing that the planning stage of Project D would take some time, he decided to finish packing what he would need for the immediate future, then work on the phone, car, and place to stay, preferably in that order. He counted the money Al and Mr. Patel had given him: $1356 from Al, which was a little less than what Charlie earned in a month, but not by much; and $2000 from Mr. Patel, which was more than double his security deposit and last month's rent. He must not want me to raise a stink about getting evicted without warning, Charlie figured, or else he's also secret friends with my Mom, seems like nearly everyone else is. Like Grady! Yes, surely Grady could get him a car, and then he could go get a motel room and start planning. Oh and a phone, he needed a phone. How had he lived these last 8 months without a cell phone? Just fine, of course, as he always argued to Emily, and to any of his friends, or anyone who would listen: phones are tools, you can't let tools decide who you are, because tools are stupid. But they were useful tools, and he would sure need to use one these next few months, until he got settled. Or in case he never did.

He put $1000 back in the small envelope and zipped it into a small knapsack, put the rest of the money in his suitcase in a plastic baggie, and went out to catch the bus. Pearson had a fairly good mass transit system for a small town, which is to say, there were 3 bus lines, and the buses ran every 2 hours or so. The fact that the bus pulled up to the stop less than 5 minutes after Charlie arrived heartened him, he took it as another sign, another indication that everything was going to be just fine, never mind that some guy the police seemed actually scared of may be driving around looking for him. The bus came. Charlie boarded. It was dark, early evening, a nice breeze had cooled the earth, and everything was going to be just fine.

He got off the bus a block from Grady's collision shop and realized a cell phone was the first thing he should have bought so he could have called Grady and told him he was on his way, since the shop was closed, and dark, and the neighborhood it occupied was made up of broken angles, pocked concrete, mounds of metal rusted into shapelessness. The dark streets squeaked and rattled loud as a harbor as Charlie walked up and peered in the front window, shading is eyes with both hands. A light was on in the back, the office door was closed but he could still see a yellow line running around its frame, so he banged on the front door. The noise echoed off the buildings behind him, so he stepped back and looked up and down the street, sure he had woken a throng of undead, or at least a gangbanger or two. Did Pearson have street gangs? He remembered hearing about a bunch of skinheads beating up some trustafarians at a concert once, but never anything about actual gangs, with colors and all that stuff. Still, if they existed, this is where they'd be, and they'd hear him banging, carrying $1000 dollars around in a little back pack, and—he heard the door's lock crackle, then saw Grady behind it. He was wearing a t-shirt and a dirty pair of boxers and a small gold crucifix on a chain around his neck, and nothing else. "The fuck, Charlie? Whatchyou want?" he sounded almost drunk, and mad about not being all the way there yet.

"Hey Grady, I'm sorry, sorry, it's late I know but I really need a car I got cash and—"

"Hold on, hold on, goddamn..." Grady turned and walked into the dark station office. "Come on, then," he called to Charlie, switching on a desk lamp and slumping down into an ancient swivel chair. Charlie nodded to himself and went and sat down opposite Grady.

"I need a car. I know it's late—"

"Yeah, yeah, all that stuff, what you need a car for?"

"Ah, well, my truck is totalled, and, well, I need to get out of town for a while."

Grady raised his eyebrows, lowered them again, and stood up. He walked through the door Charlie had first noticed the light shining from, banged around inside, and emerged a few seconds later with two cans of Keystone Light. He handed one to Charlie, then opened his own as he slumped once more into his chair.

"What happen to your truck? I sold you that truck."

"Yeah you did, it was a great truck, but, um, someone fucked it up. I mean really fucked it up."

"Why someone want to do a thing like that?"

"I don't know, kids maybe, I guess. It was, they torched it. Fire trucks and everything."

Grady raised his eyebrows again, then let them fall as he pulled on his beer.

"And now you got to get out of town."

"Yeah, for a while, just go somewhere and start again, you know? Maybe have an adventure, I don't know, the open road, driving west probably." Grady pushed forward in the chair and narrowed his eyes.

"The fuck you say. Goin' west, lookin' for adventure."

"Yeah, and so I kinda need a car now, so I can get going. I got cash, I just need a car to get there."

"So, someone set fire to your truck, and suddenly you got a bug to go west, a big ass bug makes you knock on my door at 10:30 at night, and you say you got no idea who mighta torched it? What kinda fool I look like to you?"

Charlie let his breath come rushing out. He hadn't noticed he was holding it.

"I know, I know. You've always been straight with me. I don't know what's wrong with me. I think sometimes I'm living two lives, or like I'm over here looking at myself, like there's the me that does stuff, and the me that watches me do stuff. Fuck, I sound crazy."

"Yeah, you do. So you put your truck on fire and watch yourself do it?"

"No, no. It was Derek Cavuto." Grady's rolled his eyes and shook his head.

"Now I told you to stay away from that man, I—"

"I know, you did, everyone did, but I didn't listen, and now I need a car to get the hell out of here."

Grady sat very still, drained the last of his beer, and sat very still again. Charlie listened to Grady breathe, watched him stare at his beer can. Someone blasting a subwoofer drove up the street and past the station. The throbbing noise faded away, and Charlie could hear Grady breathing again. They sat that way for a while. "Ok, let's go," Grady said suddenly, rising and flinging the beer can at the wall in one motion. He grabbed a flashlight off the desk and headed for the front door. Charlie followed.

Behind the station were several cars, several half-cars, and an old panel truck with no hood or doors. Grady shined a light on the nearest vehicle, a black Acura with a cracked windshield and rust along the wheel wells. "This one'll getcha gone. Don't look like much, but the engine good, tranny good, new belts on her, I been fixin' her up to sell her. Gimme five hundred and don't ever let me see your face again."

Charlie walked around and tugged on the door. It was locked.

"Can I look inside?"

"Look inside? Look inside? You are one presumptuous son of a bitch, you know that? Look inside. Come round my place, 10:30 at night..." Grady continued as he pushed past Charlie and unlocked the door, "tell me you got one of the Cavutos after you and gotta get outta town, and then ask me can I see inside. There, motherfucker, look inside!" He shook his head and backed away. Charlie nodded and pulled open the door. No interior light came on, but Charlie saw that it looked like, well, the inside of an old Acura. No dead dogs, but it did smell like vomit. "Wow, smells like puke."

"That's 'cause folks puked in it. I forgot to lock it when I got it and found a crackhead sleeping in it next day. He puked all over the backseat. You can go buy a little Christmas tree at the Pump'n'Pantry, once you gimme $500 and get the hell out my sight."

"Ok, ok, I got the cash, let's go in so you can count it and be sure I'm not cheating, since I'm crazy and stuff, never can tell." Back inside the station, Grady gave Charlie the keys and an inspection tag and some dealer plates. "You tell your Momma the shit you got into?" Grady asked him.

"No, not yet," Charlie sighed.

"You be right by her, you go tell her what's goin on, and when you get to where you goin, you let her know. Me, I don't want to know."

"I will. Thanks, Grady."

"You be careful. Stupid motherfucker."

Charlie drove back toward his apartment to pick up the rest of his travelling gear. He liked the way that sounded, "travelling gear," like he was heading for the Amazon in a biplane. The Acura sounded a little like a biplane, actually; the engine seemed smooth enough, but there must have been a hole in the muffler somewhere. Never mind, he was off, or nearly off, and leaving was always exciting, out into the unknown, nothing but potential, new worlds and new stories just beyond the next hill. He lost himself as he drove, let his mind graze through all the places he would go like he was flipping through a copy of National Geographic at the dentist's office. He wandered so far that he drove past his apartment, and only realized he had passed it when he saw he had driven, instinctively, to the front entrance to Pearson College. Oh well, he laughed to himself, guess I should say goodbye to you, you joke of a school. I have lots of goodbyes to say, don't I? Don't I? He turned around and headed back toward his apartment. No, he thought, I don't have many goodbyes to say at all. Goodbyes are for people who mark time, counting down the days, making notches in a stick while they sat on the porch wondering if anything would ever happen. You have to make things happen, Charlie muttered at the red light, and noted with pleasure how his words turned the light green.

CHAPTER 7

After loading his car, sweeping the kitchen, and settling down for his last night in the bed he'd shared with Emily, Charlie was seized with a panic: what if the bastard comes back! What if he trashes my car too, then I'm fucked! I can't sleep here! And so he didn't, driving instead to the Royal Arms Motel, which leaned dully at the edge of town near the entrance to the interstate. He gave thirty dollars to a witchy looking woman swaying beneath a muumuu on the other side of the counter, moved a few of his things into room eleven, and fell asleep with the TV on. When he woke, the sun was leaking through the blinds in four or five different spots where the slats were cracked. The alarm clock glowed red: 6:43.

Charlie rolled over and prodded the TV volume higher with the remote control. He hadn't watched television in a very long time, but he'd never really cared much for most of what was on; his Mom only got a set when Charlie was nine, not because he'd asked, but because she'd been seized with a compulsion to watch *Twin Peaks*. Charlie had seen TV at friend's houses before that, but he was more interested in running around, and throwing balsa wood airplanes, and making little dioramas out of figures from magazines in old shoe boxes. Once his Mom got the set, he fell into the habit of watching, and watched enough to know what his classmates talked about before the bell rang, but it never really took, the cathode addiction. He flipped around, stopping to watch the headlines spill out of CNN: John Kerry was running behind Bush in the polls, which shocked Charlie a bit since he'd forgotten all about the election, despite it's omnipresence on the internet whenever he went to McDonald's to surf. Ah well, there's no way a majority of people in this country are stupid enough to elect a half-wit, war-mongering criminal yet again, he reasoned. Hell, the next story was about how "well" things were going in Iraq, which is to say, not very well at all, and then Don Rumsfeld came on the screen licking his lizard lips and Charlie could take no more, and he poked the TV off spitefully and slid out of bed. He remembered he needed a map, he didn't even know where he was going, but he would need a map, and a phone. Phone first, downtown, then a map. And then there was Project D. He felt an electric shudder in his hands, looked and saw they were visibly shaking, spasming, even getting longer, his fingers stretching—he shook them both very hard, and saw sparks fly out and disappear in the brown grunge of the carpet. Cool.

But not cool, I could start a fire... he began stomping at the spots in the carpet where the sparks had landed, stopped in mid-stomp as it dawned on him how stupid he looked, and instead quickly pulled on his clothes. The morning light struck him full on, and he felt a twinge of his old problem with heat, then felt a greater twinge as he remembered the lengths he'd gone to avoiding heat, why someone had not stuck him deep in an asylum was hard to figure. But he'd kept his job, was a good regular tax-paying American citizen, so there, and what that fuckhead had done to his truck, that was great truck, the a/c was a thing of beauty, hard and sure and loud enough to make his ears hum.

He decided to go back in his room to lay down and think more about where he really wanted to go, and woke again near noon, angry with himself for falling asleep. He splashed water on his face and went outside, where it was warm but slightly overcast. As he opened the door to his brand new used car, he pulled the list out of the breast pocket of his shirt: "Phone, Map, Project D," was written on it with thick black marker. The heat actually feels kind of nice, he thought, and stood for moment with the open car door cradling his ass, his face absorbing the morning light. A green Subaru pulled into the space next to Charlie's car, and Charlie watched as Beth, the grad student he talked with at Greg and Mo's party, climbed out of the passenger's seat, opened the back door, and rummaged around. The driver's side door opened, and Greg stepped out, turned away from Charlie to lock the door, then turned around and froze as he saw Charlie standing there. "Wow," he said, after trying to hide by remaining perfectly still had failed. "Wuh—um, hi Charlie." Charlie felt love for Greg gushing out of the ends of his hair, he wanted to protect him, wrap him tight, he seemed so vulnerable, so fragile and gawky, like a baby bird fallen too soon from the nest.

"Greg!" Charlie said, and knew at once he'd said it too loud. "I mean, hi Greg! This is a nice motel."

"Yeah, I, it is, real nice." Greg turned and looked at Beth, who was squinting at Charlie. He did not want to wrap her tight and protect her, she seemed just fine, even a little scary. Her face was made of two faces, or maybe three, joined at sharp angles, and the light it sent out demanded something of Charlie.

"What's up?" Beth asked Greg.

"Hi Beth, I remember you, it's me, Charlie, from Mo's birthday party," Charlie answered, when it seemed Greg was not ready to speak. Beth's face shifted in a funny way, like bits of glass falling through the air, and then she gave a wry little smile and laughed. "Oh yeah. Hi Charlie. Say hi to Charlie, Greg."

"I did already, say hi, to Charlie," Greg said quietly.

"So where are you going?" Beth asked, hefting a knapsack onto her shoulder and walking around the front of Greg's car till she was on the sidewalk in front of Charlie.

"Oh, to get a phone! And a map, and, yeah."

Beth squinted at him again. "Your phone shit the bed?"

"No," Charlie said, suddenly feeling sheepish, "I just don't have one anymore. I don't know what happened to mine, actually. I guess I just let the plan expire and then forgot."

"Really," she said, and looked back at Greg, who had turned back to his car and was unlocking the car again. "What are you doing?" she said to him.

"I'm, I really don't think, we should get going, we just stopped to check the place out, Charlie, we—just checking it out," he fumbled, and finally succeeded in pulling his door open.

"Are you fucking kidding me?" Beth said, loudly. Her whole body was made of angles now, Charlie saw. Her hip was a closed jacknife.

"Come on Beth, get in the car," Greg called.

"No fucking way, you chickenshit. I fucking knew it," she barked, then turned and started down the sidewalk toward the rental office. Charlie told himself to stop grinning, he knew he shouldn't be smiling , staring at Greg, who was staring at Beth, who was at the door of the rental office, yanking it open. But he kept on grinning as Greg smacked his steering wheel and drove slowly away, never looking back at Charlie, at the gash in his face that his teeth showed through. As soon as his car slid out onto the road, Charlie felt his mouth relax, and it dawned on him why Greg and Beth were at the motel, and why they had reacted to Charlie's presence the way they had: they were planning a surprise party for him, to say goodbye and wish him well. As soon as he figured it out, he started jogging toward the rental office, and was almost there when Beth burst through the door again, shaking her head. Her angles had all merged and softened, Charlie noted.

"Can you believe they won't give me my money back? Can you believe I fucking paid for the room? Fuckity fuck fuck fuck, what's wrong with me," she finished with a mutter and stood, hip cocked in front of Charlie, staring at the ground. She didn't look angular at all anymore, she looked like a child who was trying to look tough. She sure wasn't here to give him a surprise party, Charlie realized. "You want to go get a cup of coffee? I could sure use one," he asked her. When she looked up from the sidewalk through her bangs, he saw she was about to cry. "Yeah, ok," she answered.

"Come on, I'll buy," he said, and started walking toward the dingy brick red Pump-n-Pantry that sat next to the motel, gas pumps at the ready. They walked quietly side-by-side, and as they swung their legs over a mangled parking fence, Charlie noticed this was the same Pump-n-Pantry where he had stopped for beer before going to Greg and Pat's party, and then meeting Beth. Weird, he thought, so many threads all winding together. They each bought enormous cups of stale coffee, Beth doctoring hers with a fistful of flavored creamers, Charlie with more sugar packets than he could count, and went outside to a metal picnic table that sat on a slab beside the tire air pump. Beth took a sip of her coffee and made a face. "Boy this is bad coffee," she said.

"Ha, yeah, it's amazingly bad." Charlie took a sip of his and screwed his face into scowl. It must have been a funny scowl, as Beth managed a laugh. He knew she wanted to talk, could see her skin glimmering like there were secrets trying to shine their way out of her body. So, he did the only thing he could think of: he told her why he was at the motel, and about Cavuto, and about Emily, and about everything that had happened, right up to and including the sparks that flew out of his hands onto the carpet a short time ago. He did leave out any mention of Project D, and he didn't go into details about the dead dog, just that something very bad had been done to him and his truck. When finally stopped talking, he felt like he had shed several layers of skin. He noticed the temperature rising again, the clouds had moved away, it was very hot for early September, and that Beth had a strange look on her face, equal parts curiosity (the eyebrows furrowing) and fear (her mouth tight and small and white around the edges). She was staring, which made him very conscious of his spine, and its connections to the rest of his body, its hinges, all the spots that had swelled with metallic fury in recent days, now cold. He started to shiver, despite the heat.

"That is, wow." Beth looked out across the parking lot, and Charlie stopped shivering the minute her head turned. When she looked back at him, he saw that her face was angles again, and he smiled. "Yes, that's my story and I'm sticking to it," he said.

"Man, I thought my life was fucked up," she answered. "So, your girlfriend—"

"Emily. Ex-girlfriend," Charlie said, failing to stifle a giggle at the end.

"Emily, ok, she died of what now?" Beth fished in her purse and drew out a cigarette.

"A brain aneurysm."

"Yikes, that sucks. And then you started to read all these books..."

"Yes, piles of them."

"Right, became a semi-hermit or whatever, working and reading and hiding in your house. Ok," she stopped and lit her cigarette and inhaled; "and then you got in a fight with an ice cream man who is really some kind of super criminal."

"Right."

"And now you feel like you have some kind of metal or energy growing in your bones—"

"Metal is closer, really."

"Ok, metal, and now you're going to skip town in a used Acura, and you don't even know where you're going."

"Correct! Tell her what she's won, Bob."

"That is ... " she dragged on her cigarette again and stared at a group of girl scouts who had descended from a bus into the Pump-n-Pantry. "That's just crazy, you know that, right?"

"I do! I mean, the whole chain of events is pretty weird..."

"And the shit about metal growing on your spine, you know that is seriously crazy, right? Like, you think you're Wolverine or something? That's not right, Charlie. That's scary."

Charlie thought for a minute. "I'm a Wolverine, what?"

Beth stopped in mid-inhale and coughed. "That is even more scary. You don't know who Wolverine is? Seriously?" Charlie shook his head, and Beth stubbed out her half-smoked cigarette. He looked past her at the dirty wall of the gas station, and then at the entrance to the interstate beyond. He could be anywhere. He was anywhere. As he watched, a mini-van pulled up to one of the pumps, and a nun in full regalia got out and started to pump gas. When he looked back, Beth was crying, motionless, silent. Something in his chest snapped like a fishing line breaking, and he felt her sadness rush into the space where the tautness had been. He hadn't even known the tension was there, and now it was gone, and he felt his eyes begin to spill too, down his cheeks. "He's a fucker, he always has been, Greg, I mean," he said, knowing it was not helpful, but hoping at least to break their tears.

"Well, that's what I was hoping," she replied, and sniffled and chortled at once, which impressed Charlie deeply.

"Yeah, he always cheats on everyone. That's what I tried to tell—"

"Forget it, Charlie, that's not why I'm crying. You really never heard of Wolverine?" she pulled her spine straight and pressed her fingertips together.

"You're crying because I don't know who Wolverine is?"

"No, dumb-ass, I'm trying to change the subject. Tell you what, you give me a ride back downtown, and I'll show you who Wolverine is."

Charlie smiled and wiped his face. "Ok, bet."

They drove slowly and made fun of what was on the radio. Beth had Charlie stop and buy a *Wolverine* anthology at the comic store, and they ate sandwiches and drank a pitcher of beer at a tavern and she flipped through the book until she found the page she wanted, then plopped it down in front of him and went to the bathroom. The story was absurd, Charlie saw, a government conspiracy to create super-soldier that involved, among other things, fusing this Wolverine guy's bones with a made-up metal called Adamantium. "That's pretty silly shit," Charlie said, when Beth returned, "but the art is cool."

"Of course it's silly, if the government was that bad-ass we'd all be remotely controlled or something, or nests for space aliens," she laughed.

Charlie raised an eyebrow. "I like the way you think," he said, and went back to reading.

As he dropped her off in front of the apartment she shared with her sister, he felt he should try to kiss her, or hug her, or maybe just raise his eyebrow again, he didn't know quite what he was supposed to do. When she turned in her seat to say goodbye, he took her hand and kissed that, and knew by the angle of her smile that he'd chosen correctly, or at least not as badly as he could have. She even called "let's go do something again sometime, when you get back," through the open window of the car as he put it into gear, and he waved. He went to mall, bought and activated a new cell phone, then headed toward the hardware store to get the supplies he would need for project D, the whole time feeling as if his body had no edges, no matter, that he extended beyond the pull of gravity, down through the earth, out into space, in all directions. The feeling persisted as he loaded his trunk with cans of road paint, flares, a gas can, a box of rags, one hundred feet of nylon rope, a box of safety matches, and two six packs of Mountain Dew, which was on sale, two for five dollars.

CHAPTER 8

Finding the place the ice cream trucks came and went from was easy enough, one google search from his table at McDonald's told Charlie that there was only one ice cream novelty distributor in Pearson, which was not surprising, and that it was a few blocks from Grady's garage, which also made perfect sense, given the shambolic state of the neighborhood in question. Ten minutes later, Charlie parked across the street from Mr. Cool's Novelties, in a little half-alley between an abandoned building and a vacant lot overseen by the canopies of two huge oak trees. He drank Mountain Dew and played with his new phone and read the newspaper, watching various cars and trucks that were not made for selling ice cream drive in and out the front gate. After three Mountain Dews, he was ready to pee, so he went out behind his car and pissed on the wall, looking over at the gate just in time to catch sight of a late model, powder blue Mercedes Benz as it pulled out through the gate and headed north. Jumping back into the car and zipping his pants at the same time he managed to catch some of his pubic hair in the zipper, so he let out a yelp as he sat down, the hair tearing as the zipper pushed away from his lap. He followed the Benz as discretely as he could, scenes from cop shows and gangster movies flitting through his head... and then floating out the top, as his skull suddenly felt like it had no crown, as though the top of it had simply dissolved and his thoughts were now free to expand upward, out into the universe. The Benz went back through downtown Pearson, past the college, and out to a dull, if well-heeled, suburb, marked by a sign nestled amidst a clump of hostas and marigolds as "Regency Meadows." They turned onto Pinewood, then onto Willowalk, and then onto

Lower Woodberry Court, at which point Charlie knew he would never, ever find his way out of here on his own. The Benz slowed and pulled into the driveway of a pale yellow, split-level house and parked next to a black Jeep Cherokee. There were toys scattered in the yard, and Charlie watched as Derek Cavuto climbed out of the Benz, hefted a paper bag from the passenger's side, and kicked at a red plastic tricycle parked in the path to the front door. The trike fell off the path into the landscaping, and Charlie drove on past until he came to a cul-de-sac. As he followed the circle around, he saw a woman with a long braid kneeling in a small garden in front of one of the houses, and she seemed to be crying. He stopped and looked back in his rear view mirror at her, hunched, shaking, then she stood up and he saw that she was not crying but yelling into a cell phone.

What to do? What was the plan? Plan D, "d" for Derek, "d" for dickhead, "d" for die you fuckwad. No, not dead, Charlie shook his head. I just want him to be sad. I want him to feel what I have felt, which is not much because everything is so far away, people yelling into cell phones or crying into them or making great theatrical scenes from their lives, people dead for no good reason on the kitchen floor and it's just a body, it's so simple, such an easy relationship: person minus life equals just a body, even person plus life is mostly just a body, this body I'm wearing now, the one surging and crackling in anticipation, like the one my Dad wore and did crazy shit with but not for me to see or know about, the one Beth wears that bends and curves just so and just so right it makes me want to see how my body fits hers.

The sun was turning orange and shadows were starting to seep between the vinyl-sided buildings. Charlie sat at the cusp of the cul-de-sac, shaking, squeezing the steering wheel. He wondered what his mother was doing, if she was folding laundry or dancing around the living room to the Ramones or biting her nails at the kitchen table, worrying about him. She would not like to know where he was, what he was planning, but he knew she would also not want him to let it go, she would want him to stand up for himself. He remembered a spring day when he was ten or eleven years old and the police brought him home from the playground, handcuffed. Some older boys had been throwing rocks through the middle school windows, and Charlie and his friends were watching and laughing, and Charlie ran the wrong way when the police appeared out of thin air. He wouldn't tell them who was throwing the rocks, so the cops cuffed him and drove around for a while, trying to scare him. It worked, but he knew that ratting would only make things worse, and then they brought him home and his mother screamed at the policemen, threatened them, her face a strange, dark flurry that fell into tears as soon as they left, apologizing, bowing, even. He never forgot that face, it visited his nightmares for years. She would not want him to let his life be yanked from beneath him by some suburban ice cream goon.

It was night now, and Charlie didn't remember turning off the car, or how long he'd been sitting at the side of the road. He looked at his phone: 9:49 p.m. He'd sat there for more than 2 hours. That no one had called the police on him was a wonder. Maybe people just didn't look outside much around here, didn't see a skinny, swarthy little man with a bad glow in his eyes hunched over the wheel of a shitty car that clearly did not belong to a resident of Regency Meadows. He started the car and drove slowly down the street, leaving the headlights off, as that is what stealthy people do, he thought. The picture window at the front of Derek Cavuto's house glowed with a weirdly greenish light, and Charlie eased past and parked at the curb in front of the house next to Cavuto's. He felt suddenly suspended, weightless, as though all the strange twists and turns, all the bad decisions, even the good ones, were threads lifting him up and out through the roof of his car, up into the night sky. The battered Acura sat dully beneath him at the curb. One of the books he'd read was about this kind of thing, one of the books he'd read but he couldn't remember which, they were an indistinguishable mass in his head, one of those clumps of text archeologists find in garbage heaps and have to x-ray to pick out the glyphs, but he had no x-ray, no way to tell if he had read about out-of-body experiences, or if he'd had them before, or if he was crazy, or if his insanity was inventing Charlie Price out of whole cloth. Then he was back in the car, feeling as stupid and as self-indulgent as all the people he hated so, all the old men and women wandering around wondering why the world hadn't turned out as they expected, all the scrabbling middle aged fools clinging to the idiot songs they sang when they were young, all the young cattle herding themselves down the ramp, behaving like crude puppets all the while thinking it their birthright. Even the children were not innocent, only lacking knowledge; if this world is a penal colony, then the children are closest to the crimes that landed them here, and they haven't learned how to forget, they're fresh meat, fresh meat, and Charlie was up and out of the car, singing it to himself, "fresh meat, fresh meat," opening the trunk and taking out the gas and the rags and paint, singing to himself and laughing when he heard the tune he was trying to bend the words to was "Music Box Dancer," of course of course, and the smell of the gas bloomed in his nostrils as he poured it on the Benz and the Cherokee, it bloomed in his veins and he felt metallic clouds washing through his body and lit a safety match on the driveway and tossed it. He sprayed paint wildly, toward the burst of flame and toward the grass and up in the sky and laughed again, his Wolverine bone-energy was gone, wiped away in waves of gas and paint and he turned the spray can at his head and filled his hair with paint and reached down for the half empty gas can, "fresh meat, fresh meat," the car all at once catching fire and then an idea came to him but it wasn't an idea, it was his head suddenly cracking open and then it cracked again and he went down.

"So, we put him in the river."

"Can't put him in the fucking river, how many fucking people saw this guy on your front lawn doing a fire dance? How many saw you knock his ass out and drag it inside? How many saw the cops show up and leave without him, how many? The fucking river. Jesus you're sloppy."

"Don't worry about the neighbors, I told them all—"

"Don't worry about the neighbors? What the fuck, why do you live in that fucking place anyway, what kind of gangster lives in a goddamn suburb? How you gonna get respect from anybody living in Doucheville?"

"Sylvia likes it there, come on, don't start this shit with me again. And I ain't a fucking gangster."

"Oh yeah right, you're a businessman, you're fucking straight as they come, you wanted to put this guy in the river and now—"

"No, I—"

"Shut the fuck up. Wake this cocksucker, he stinks like gas."

"I ain't a fucking gangster because no one uses that word anymore except niggers, Pop. Right Zook?"

"I hadn't really checked, Mr. C."

"Hadn't really checked. When was the last time you called yourself a gangster?"

"Don't refer to myself in terms of my vocation in many conversations at all, Mr. C."

Charlie's head cracked again, this time as white light shot through his eyes into his skull. He had something in his mouth, pressing his tongue down against the floor of his mouth. He blinked and tried to rub his eyes but his arms were tied behind his back, tied around a chair, as were his feet, as he discovered while trying to wriggle free. The world slowly emerged from the white light, and Derek Cavuto stood off to the left of his field of vision, arms crossed, leaning back against what looked like cheap wood paneling. Beside him a squat, orange man with heavy eyebrows sat in a plush green chair, and beside him, a large man with a blank face stood, placid as a brick. A wooden desk fringed in the same green as the plush chair sat between Charlie and the orange man, and on the desk were scraps of paper, balled up tissues, and several empty single-serving cereal boxes, along with a brass statue of a bucking horse and rider. The rider held his hat to his head with his hand. "Hiya princess," said the orange man. Charlie squinted, and shook his head. He really was orange, the kind of orange tanning addicts eventually turn, but even more vivid, so that when he sat back in his chair, Charlie saw trails of orange smear backwards from his face.

"Take that fucking thing out of his mouth, Zook, how's our guest supposed to answer questions?"

The large man, who was, Charlie noticed, impeccably tailored in a silver-grey suit, walked past Charlie's right ear, and Charlie felt a tug at the back of his head, then something fell from his mouth. His jaw ached, his head was throbbing, and the smell of gasoline was everywhere, in his eyes, in his ears, in between his veins. The large man dropped a wet red ball hanging from a leather strap on the corner of the desk. Charlie coughed, and then could not stop coughing, it felt as though a tick had attached itself to the back of his throat and was rubbing its belly against his flesh. Something twinkled at the corner of his vision. He stopped, and felt a tail of spit chilling on his chin, down onto his neck.

"Oh, princess, you are a mess," the orange man said. Derek winced as he spoke, and shook his head at Charlie. "So, why don't you tell me a story," the orange man continued.

"Well, I,—" Charlie's voice sounded like it was coming from somewhere else in the room, from a speaker phone hidden in a cereal box. "I just learned about Wolverine."

The orange man cocked his head, then turned his cocked head toward Derek. Derek shrugged.

"Tell me, princess, a story about how you came to be on my son-in-law's front lawn, in his very respectable neighborhood, setting his car on fire. That's the story I want to hear."

Charlie told them the story, starting with the song of the ice cream truck and ending with the smell of gasoline. The orange man, who would be dead three weeks later after choking on a piece of his toenail—the second destructive result of his unfortunate lifelong habit of biting said nails, the first being a divorce from his first, best wife—could barely contain his laughter when Charlie described fishing his shit out of the toilet and flinging it at Derek, even crying a bit in his mirth. His face went red when Charlie described his plan to burn Derek's cars, house, and person, and as soon as he sensed Charlie was through talking, he stood up from behind the desk, walked around to Charlie, and punched him as hard as he could on the side of his jaw. It hurt his hand, his knuckles were out of shape. He turned and leaned against the desk, shaking his head and staring vaguely at the horse statue.

"Boss. Boss. Sit down a minute," Zook said, and guided the orange man back to his seat.

"When I think of how this shitbag... he could've killed children, my granddaughters, my Sylvia! What the fuck, she don't need this shit, it'll send her into remission..."

"He's a sick tool, boss. The man plays with his shit. So, let's figure it out," Zook purred. He was the only man in the room who had actually ever worked for the Mafia, and that was when he was a twelve year old in Brooklyn, carrying bookie slips and stashing guns around town. Then his parents moved to Pittsburgh, and Zook still lived with them, helping his mother manage his father's Alzheimer's as best they could while they both watched her own dementia seep over the horizon like a thundercloud.

"He's mine, come on, I mean shit, I should get to do this. Take care of this situation," Derek said.

"You don't take care of shit!" Orange man yelled. "You don't know enough to keep your fucking gun in your pants when some nutbag knocks on your door, you want to be all gangster now and take care of it? What my daughter ever saw in you... it wasn't fucking genius, I'll tell you that."

"How'm I supposed to know he's a nutbag? Not like he's wearing a fucking sign."

"Not the point! You listen to me—" he stood and looked up into Derek's face— "It is time for you to act like a professional. To act like a man. A man doesn't pull out a gun because some flathead asks you to turn down the tinkle truck. Unprofessional. Un-pro-fesh-un-al!"

"Yeah...." Derek looked bashful, and Charlie realized he was the same age as Derek, that Derek might even be younger.

"Yeah. You want people to respect you? To see you and know that you got power? That's what a real gangster does."

"Jesus, Pop, again with the 'gangster' thing. Where'd you get that word, anyway?"

"Tell you what, stop calling me 'Pop,' I'll stop calling us 'gangsters,' cause I'm not your fucking Pop, I'm Sylvia's Pop, I'm your goddamn boss."

Derek's face dropped. "You told me to call you that! At the wedding!"

"He's right, no one uses 'gangster' to describe themselves anymore except for some rappers," Charlie interjected. All three men fixed him with sudden, anthropological stares.

"Did he just tell me I'm not a gangster?" orange man said.

"It's not the right word. If you were Mafia, you would be 'made,' or a 'wiseguy' or something, so I guess you aren't Mafia. You could call yourself 'crooks,' but that's too cartoonish. 'Desperado' is too westerny, and then there's that awful Eagles song—wait, is that an oxymoron? Hahaha!—Maybe you could bring 'brigand' back, or even 'highwayman,' provided you have something to do with roads, do you guys do any road robberies or whatchacall, hijacking? That might be cool, actually, kinda retro, you could wear leather hats, not horses of course but maybe motorcycles—no, scooters! Vespas, yeah, and fingerless gloves and mmph—" Zook shoved the rubber ball back in his mouth and pulled the strap tight.

"What the fuck was that all about? Is he on something?" orange man asked. Derek and Zook both shrugged. "Get him out of here," he added. Zook nodded and tilted Charlie in his chair and rolled him backward out of the room. It was the first time he noticed that he was strapped into a wheelchair.

After Zook closed the door behind him, Derek sat on the corner of the desk. "I'm asking a favor here, Pop. Let me take care of this loser. Like you said, he coulda killed my babies."

"Nope. How many witnesses? How many people saw you crack his skull? Saw your damn CAR on fire? You gotta stay out of it. We'll let Brandon take care of him."

"Brandon? Oh man, he's a fucking idiot..."

"Yes, Brandon. You want to say something bad about Brandon? I known Brandon a lot longer than I known you, kid. Knew him since he was in diapers" He tilted his chair back against the wall. "You call him. Call him and tell him to scare the shit out of this—what's his fucking name, anyway?"

"Charlie Price," Derek answered.

"Charlie? Ha, that's funny, I don't know why. So tell Brandon to scare him, make him cry, make him into a little girl, but nothing too physical, don't break nothing, don't leave marks. Well, not many."

"But—he tried to set my house on fire! I wanna put his ass in the river!"

"Shut up. This is too hot right now. You do like I say, have Brandon scare him good—you don't think he can scare this kid? That's about the only thing Brandon is good at, fuck, he scares me sometimes—and then later, much later, if he hasn't offed himself, then you can do your business. We got big things coming up, this is not the time to be fucking around with some college kid. I can't believe you got yourself in this situation. The Jamaicans are coming in next week, Arnie's crew is coming in October, this is how you make the big-time, kid, and once you do, then you can squash little pricks like Charlie Price and not worry about a stink."

Charlie enjoyed being wheeled backwards out of the office, seeing the walls and furniture slide away behind the doorway, the staring and sneering faces of Derek and orange man wiped out by the edge of the door closing. He even felt happy, or at least relieved, as he was shuttled down a short dark hallway and parked in a small, nearly empty room near an elevator, because he had sense that everything would be resolved very soon, that they would kill him momentarily and so rather than panic, he felt a kind of freedom, and a quiet elation. He thought he might feel even better without the ball in his mouth, which was now making him drool, and the drool was turning cold.

When Zook returned, he carried with him a small leather satchel, which he set on a low table Charlie hadn't noticed before, just past where his left arm was lashed to the arm of the wheelchair. While Charlie strained to see, Zook unzipped the satchel, took out a syringe, and thrust it competently into the vein inside Charlie's elbow. Charlie's head began to ooze, days and years that had been clamped to his brain fell away like the shells of locusts blasted from the underside of a lawn chair with a hose. "Mmnnhh," he said, and Zook went around to unhook the strap holding the ball secure in Charlies mouth. "Mmnnhh, " he said again, this time with his mouth not quite as open, and half smile drawing over his face. "That's right, princess, sweet dreams," Zook said, and left him there, throbbing incandescently, dreaming, the world behind his eyes shimmering like the surface of a dead sea.

CHAPTER 9

Charlie faded in and out of time, watched it drift away from his outstretched hand, stopped trying to grasp it... time is a quality of mind, he told himself, especially if the mind in question is suffused with psychoactive substances. Pure realization of this point, a sudden awareness that the slog of minutes, the wheel of Samsara grinding everything down, has been cast aside, that we exist outside of the quality of mind that entraps and defines us, even as it emerges from our neurons, might be the most important reason human beings take drugs in the first place. Speed makes you faster than time, narcotics make it slow enough as to seem irrelevant, alcohol turns it into a hydrant for pissing on, psychedelics flip it inside out and show you the source, the wormhole within. To say that Charlie had lost track of time, then, would be something of a misnomer, as he had really lost track of a need for time, and without this need, his surroundings became both more distinct and more shrouded in mystery, as if the connection between him and the walls of the room where he sat, tied to a wheelchair, had changed properties. He could be in a coffin and the walls would still be as pleasant to look at, the very correct way that they met with the floor and with each other, the lines they made, the shadows they made. It was all very proper, and put him in mind of an informal English country breakfast, of a maid bringing trays of rashers and hot coffee, of shining utensils for every possible circumstance, of words used with decorum and grace, the newspaper also brought in a on a shining silver tray, talk of the weather and the state of things, which, while worrisome, was as well as could be expected.

Slowly he drifted into wakefulness and temporality, didn't remember falling asleep, and didn't feel so fine anymore, though a great fog did remain, as did his arm restraints, as did the wheelchair. He felt the chair leap and buck beneath him, and the walls of the room crashed loudly, metallically, and all at once it dawned on him that he was in the back of an empty panel truck. He faded back, his eyes sank, his thoughts spun this time a panorama of women, girls, old, young, all unclothed, heads flung back in ecstasy, their sleek legs, their breasts swaying and resting on his forehead, a swan neck here ending in a curve of shoulder, here a bushy eyebrow raised above an eye smiling darkly. It had been a long time since he thought of women this way, a very long time, and he saw Beth and the smooth angles of her body unfolding beneath him, and he saw Emily clinging to him, her legs digging into his kidneys, and he saw Maryanne, his first college girlfriend, her nails flecked with black polish where she hadn't chewed them off, her mouth cold and tasting of sausage but her thighs: engines of true mercy. It had been a long time, he hadn't even masturbated since, when,—and before he could remember he came, a cold wet spot growing on the inside leg of his jeans. I've had a waking wet dream, he thought, and sank further into the fog, below words, below the spot where shape emerged from nothingness.

The door of the truck ratcheting open snapped him awake, and the night outside seemed as dark as the inside of the truck. A flashlight danced around the walls and settled on his face, and he heard voices, and felt someone climb into the back of the truck. "Hello, darling," Zook said as he bent down and unhooked the straps on the floor that kept the wheelchair from sliding around.

"Hi, sweetie," Charlie answered. Zook stopped and shone the flashlight in Charlie's eyes again, then punched him hard in the mouth. Charlie felt his teeth hum like someone had touched a tuning fork to each one . He rubbed his tongue over his gums and felt blood, but none of the teeth seemed loose or missing. Zook rolled Charlie to the end of the truck and down the ramp, the wheels making metallic hissing noises as they descended. He kept on rolling him through the dark, and as Charlie's eyes adjusted, he saw he was in some kind of warehouse. A door, set in a corrugate metal wall, grew out of the darkness, and they stopped beside it. "This is your final destination. I hope you had a pleasant journey," Zook said, bowing at the waist, before smacking Charlie on the mouth again, the same side, but not nearly as hard. Charlie heard a buzzing and looked down to see Zook's gloved hand pressing a button, then heard Zook's footsteps echoing away behind him. It occurred to him to turn his head and say something parting to Zook, but he couldn't think of any reason why he should, or any reason why he should do anything. He wriggled in his chair and noticed the clump of ejaculate in his jeans had begun to dry and glue his pants to his leg.

Time sagged again between the moment Charlie heard the panel truck start up and the moment the door opened. When the door finally did open, a tall, birdish man with a tooth missing in the front of his mouth sprung from the dark and dragged Charlie forward by the arms of the wheelchair. The man was rasping heavily, and after he had dragged Charlie fifteen feet, he disappeared again, and Charlie heard the door behind him close. A light burst on a few feet from his face, a light bright enough that he could feel the heat roaring off, making his eyelashes curl and his skin tighten. He remembered when he'd been allergic to heat, so long ago.

"Look at him," a voice said, somewhere behind the light.

"Mm-hmm, tasty," a higher pitched voice answered the first.

"I'm actually pretty tasteless," Charlie mumbled.

"What'd he say?" said the deeper voice.

"I don't know, he's drooling and shit."

"I said," Charlie held his head up into the light and barked, "I'm pretty tasteless."

There was a pause, and then the high voice spoke: "What's he talking about?"

"I don't know. Let's play with him."

"Yeah."

The light switched off, and Charlie welcomed a cool rush of air. A dimmer light flicked on somewhere ahead, and Charlie could make out the outline of another door in the distance. Someone came up behind him and shoved the chair, and soon they were at the other door, and then through the doorway into a small, dark room whose oily walls seemed filthy even in the light of a single desk lamp. The lamp sat on a battered metal desk, and behind it, the birdish man sat, opening and closing a pair of needle-nose pliers. To the right of the desk was a ratty, blue, fake leather couch, gaping with holes, on which a short but very thick man sat with one leg crossed over his knee. The smaller man had short, spiky hair, a huge mole on his temple, and a Slayer t-shirt on that looked even rattier than the couch. The birdish man wore a baseball hat. Yankees. Of course, Charlie thought.

"Welcome, captive," said the birdish man. The smaller man stared at Charlie, grinning, and then forgetting to grin every few seconds, then grinning again, like a boat's springline slackening and tautening in choppy water.

"Unnh,"Charlie felt a sudden of nausea wash up from his bowels. He realized he hadn't gone to the bathroom in a very long time.

The birdish man stood and walked around the desk, settling just behind Charlie's left ear, the lobe of which he promptly grabbed with the pliers and twisted.

"Ow fucking ow!" Charlie yelled, and the man let go.

"He's loud," said bird man.

"Way too loud," answered the wide man as he lifted himself off the couch, a roll of duct tape in his hand.

He taped Charlie's mouth shut, and watched as bird man pinched and twisted Charlie with the pliers, his ears, his nipples, the skin of his forearm. It didn't hurt much after a few minutes, and Charlie quickly stopped reacting. Then the wide man went behind the desk and got a blowtorch, and as he opened and fired it, Charlie fainted.

"Well that fucking sucks, wake him up Brandon," said the bird man.

"Nah, let's wait. We got the other one in the freezer, put him in there too, Gipper's coming with a bag, let's party first and then we'll fuck him up."

"What if he wakes up?"

"Who cares, put him in the freezer, put the sack on his head and put him in, fucking tard."

Charlie roused as the birdman jerked the wheelchair around and steered him out the back of the room and down a wide hallway. They stopped at the end of the hall beside the door to a walk in cooler, and Charlie heard the tearing sound of duct tape being peeled off the roll. Birdman wrapped another piece over Charlie's mouth and around to the back of his head, pulled open the cooler door and shoved Charlie inside, then closed the door behind him without a word. The room was not cool at all, the air was hot and thick and stale, and it smelled faintly of rot. It was also pitch black, and Charlie wobbled his head around, looking for a recognizable shape, anything but the static dark. To his left he thought he could make out a small point of light, but he couldn't be sure his mind wasn't inventing it, and then the point seemed several hundred yards away, moving slowly toward him, and he knew it couldn't be real, so he closed his eyes. "So, this is a problem," a voice said, and he opened his eyes again and saw Emily standing in the corner of the room, her hands on her hips. She was not there, he knew, wearing faded jeans with holey knees, a Dead Kennedys t-shirt, a dark blue cardigan sweater. She was not. "Yes, I'm here, Charlie, you aren't crazy, even though you've been trying hard to be. And what is up with that, anyway?" She was not a lovely woman, her nose was doughy and her eyes small and piggish, her thin blond hair hanging rattily out of the bun she wore habitually, and half-heartily, at the top of her head. She was not lovely but she woke something in Charlie's heart, and not just in his, men were drawn to her wherever they went, and Charlie could never figure out why. He remembered watching her sleep one night, drool smearing the pillow, sitting up in bed beside her with a pen and paper in hand, listing all the ways she was unattractive and all the ways she was attractive, physically, emotionally, and intellectually. The "unattractive" column went on for most of the page, and most of the scant few items on the "attractive" side were intellectual: she was incredibly smart, was curious about things, was an interesting conversationalist. Under "emotionally" he had "funny" and then had written "crazy" and then crossed it out, then wrote it under both columns, then got spooked and tore the page out of the notebook and went to the kitchen to burn it in the flame of the stove top. "Nice, I come back from the dead and all you can think about is cataloguing my faults. That's creepy, Charlie."

"Um, I think coming back from the dead and reading my fucking mind is a little more creepy," he tried to say, but the duct tape muffled the words.

"Yeah, you're right it is, but really, making a list of all the things you found unattractive about me? You're like a junior high school girl." Charlie moved his head to respond more directly to her, then thought better of it. She's not there, after all, I'm not talking to a dead person.

"Fine, silent treatment again, whatever. I'm not here to fight with you, I'm here to help. You have a serious problem, did you know that? Have you, how shall we say, fully grasped the reality of your situation?" Emily sat and crossed her legs at the knee. Charlie hadn't notice there was a chair there. He squinted, and still wasn't sure there was one.

"Ok, I'm game," he said, trying to ignore the fact that he was talking through a strip of tape. "What should I do?"

"Well, let's see. You're tied to a wheelchair, your head is wrapped in duct tape, which is really gonna hurt when they tear it off your face because you have, like, 3 days worth of beard, not to mention your hair on your head, why did they wrap it all the way around like that? And there are two losers outside waiting to kill you, or at the very least mangle you with a blow torch and some pliers. That it so far?"

"You're funny, yes," he replied.

"So, I don't know, there doesn't seem to be much you can do unless you untie yourself, then you could sneak away."

"Why don't you untie me?"

Emily sneered. "Oh, now you're funny, I'm dead, Charlie, re-member?"

"Yes, I remember."

"A brain aneurysm, right? Isn't that what you tell people, Charlie?"

"I don't want to talk about it."

"Of course not, of course not. But I do, and it doesn't look like you're in much position to stop me. So. Skyler."

Charlie's mind went blank. "What—I don't get it, what you're talking about—"

"Skyler. I was going to name it Skyler, whether it was a boy or a girl. Our baby, Charlie."

A laugh bubbled up, he couldn't help it. He knew she would be even more angry, but it came anyway. "Skyler? What kind of name is Skyler?"

"Fuck you. Fuck you, you don't fucking laugh at that. It's a per-fectly good name."

"It's fucking ridiculous, it sounds like a Disney character, or a

Swedish snack cake or something."

Emily glowered for a moment, then laughed as well. Her face blooming into laughter was one of the very attractive things, Charlie remembered, and her laugh was probably the loveliest of all.

"Ok, so that's not so good, not that it matters. It's still pretty cowardly to go around telling everyone I had a brain aneurysm."

"Well, what should I tell them?"

She stopped smiling. "Tell them I committed suicide Charlie—"

"No."

"Tell them I committed suicide by washing down a handful of oxies with a bottle of drain cleaner while you were out drinking with your friends," she went on. "Tell them I drank drain cleaner and that I was 3 months pregnant with your baby, Charlie—"

"I can't."

"And then tell them that you went out drinking, after you told me you me you were moving out and that you wanted me to get an abortion, Charlie. Tell them how you made list of all the doctors within a day's drive that would do it, so you could compare prices."

"I never told you that! Fuck...." Charlie could feel that he was crying, he didn't know when he's started.

"I found the list, Charlie, another of your fucking lists. God I was so stupid, being dead is so amazingly boring." She stood and started pacing slowly. Charlie continued crying, waves of sobs cascading over and back, over and back, until he passed out.

"Oh shit, what stinks?" A light blazed on overhead and Charlie, his head still flung back from sleep, fought the urge to open his eyes and let the light blind him. He lowered his head slowly, shook it, and squinted at the birdman, hunched in the doorway with his arm crooked over his nose and mouth.

"Jesus Christ, Brandon come here a minute. I think one if these boys made a mess."

Brandon yelled something from down the hall that Charlie couldn't make out.

"The fuck, I'm not cleaning them up, you clean them up." More yelling from down the hall. Charlie thought of the parents' voices in the *Charlie Brown Christmas* special. He tried to look around, but his neck had a knot in it thick enough to moor a cruise ship. He watched as the birdman walked toward him, bent down, and squinted at Charlie, his arm still bent over his nose. "MMMUMPHFF!!" Charlie said, shaking his head from side to side, which brought flashes of colored lights to his eyes and nearly made him pass out again. When his vision cleared, he saw that he was in fact in a meat locker, rusty hooks on a rail overhead, tiled floor and walls a tapestry of stains, two very bright overhead lamps in a row between the rails. And it did smell more than awful, how had he not noticed it before? He did, or thought he did, it smelled of shit or rotten meat, as it must have when he was shoved inside but now he felt is his stomach wrenching, pushing upwards... can't be sick, he told himself, can't puke because I will drown, it will come out my nose, I'll suffocate... "oh shit oh fuck oh shit!" birdman whined from behind Charlie's head, and Charlie strained to twist his neck. Out of the corner of his eye, he could see birdman hopping from foot to foot, holding himself, before dashing past Charlie out the door, still whining a low stream of curses. Charlie wedged his foot under the left wheelchair foot brace and lifted it enough for his foot to touch the ground, then began pushing the chair back and to the left, inching his way, focused on shifting his body to maximize the motion and to avoid vomiting. Soon he had turned almost forty five degrees to the left, and saw himself sitting in a regular wooden chair, his mouth wrapped in duct tape, his hair bushier, his skin gone gray and his chin in his chest. No, that's not me, he thought, rocking himself in the chair, first Emily and not this, I really have lost it—the clothes were different, he didn't own shirt like that, and then he was shoved backwards, hard, and hit the wall. Brandon and birdman stood a few feet from the other Charlie, bodies poised in the air, ready for action, like a high speed photographer had snapped them about to attack a wild boar. They didn't move for a very long time. "Check him, Skeech," Brandon finally said, and Skeech turned to protest, thought better of it, and put his fingers against the other Charlie's neck. "He fucking dead, Brandon, oh shit man..."

"Shut up." If Brandon had any inkling that he would one day find himself working as a janitor at the True Word megachurch in Joplin, Missouri, he might have fallen to his knees and begged God's forgiveness, but that time was a long way off, long after he accidentally killed Skeech with a flare gun and tossed his body in Lake Tionesta. He scratched the back of his head, then turned to look at Charlie. "What the fuck are you looking at?"

"Mmm...umpmmh," Charlie answered. Brandon walked quickly toward him and drew back his fist, then stopped, his eyes narrowing. He grabbed the arms of the wheelchair and yanked Charlie forward, then backed him in beside the dead Charlie. He lifted dead Charlie's head and held it up with a hand on his forehead. The smell was overpowering now, and Charlie swooned.

"Check it out," Brandon said to an uncomprehending Skeech.

"What?"

"They're like fucking twins, look at that." Skeech stretch his neck from side to side.

"Wow, that's weird. But so what? What are we gonna do? Those guys are—"

"Look at them, Skeech," Brandon interrupted, voice nearly a whisper. "Their mothers couldn't tell them apart."

"Nah, they don't look that much alike, this guy has a bigger nose, and the ears are totally different, and this guy has a mole on his forehead, and—"

"Skeech! Look! Do you think they're gonna fingerprint'em for fuck's sake? Check their DNA?"

"Do I think who is what, now?" Brandon dropped dead Charlie's forehead and got close to Skeech's ear.

"We got people coming in like an hour to pick this guy up, and we're gonna give him to them, because if we don't, what do you think will happen?"

"Very bad things."

"Yes, very bad things."

"But he's dead, they said make sure he's not dead."

"Right, but this guy's not dead, is he?" Skeech smiled slowly.

"Ah, ok, I get it. But Zook said—"

"Fuck what Zook said, who you want to deal with, Zook or the fucking Terminator and the Men In Black and shit?"

Skeech shook his head. "Man, we're fucked."

"No we're not, come on, help me," Brandon said, and pulled

Charlie away from the wall. He tugged at the duct tape on the back of Charlies' head, trying to pull the two ends apart, tearing Charlies' hair in the process. Skeech went around the other side, and suddenly the ends were free and the tape pulled away from his head and mouth and Charlie wretched, a thin jet of bile splashing on his lap. He choked out a scream and Brandon promptly slapped him hard on the side of his head. "None of that, bitch," he said, then added "bring him" as he walked quickly through the door.

Back in the front room, Brandon sat on the desk and stared at Charlie. Charlie stared back. His body roared, pain shooting up from his ankles, and his skin felt as if it were about to start cracking and flaking away. Skeech was sprawled on the couch, chewing his thumb, and Emily was sitting behind Brandon, on the desk, her legs swinging over the side, filling Charlie with the urge to giggle.

"Now you listen to me," Brandon began.

"No thanks," Charlie answered, and the giggles slipped free.

"Don't be stupid," Emily said.

"Don't be stupid," Brandon also said. "You're fucking lucky, you don't even know how lucky. My associate and I were gonna have some mad fun with you, tear your shit up, bury your parts in the woods. It was gonna be a great party. Weren't you looking forward to it, Skeech?"

"Oh yeah, highlight of my week," Skeech answered.

"That's right, we're pretty disappointed. Cause we don't get to play, and you get to stay breathing. This is how it's going to go down," he said, and leaned over to rest his elbows on his knees.

"These guys are comical," Emily said over Brandon's shoulder.

"I know," Charlie laughed. "Too much television."

Brandon followed Charlies' eyes to a spot behind him, then squinted hard. "What the fuck are you trying to do here?" Charlie smiled. It made his face ache.

"Never mind, just listen: your name is Josh Tebow. Got it? Say it with me: Josh—"

"Oshkosh mosh posh," Charlie answered. Brandon reached back and pulled out a pistol.

"Try again, motherfucker. Josh—"

"Josh. I'm really thirsty."

"Tebow."

"Tebow. I'm really—"

"I got it, give him something to drink, and give him some of that jerky in the desk, he looks like a fucking junkie. There you go, Josh, some water and some delicious beef jerky, that's your fucking gold star. If anyone asks you, your name is Josh Teblow. I mean Tebow, fuck. If you say anything else, you will be dead. Do you understand me?"

"Tell them if they kill you they'll be in big trouble," Emily said.

"If you kill me, you'll be in pretty deep shit, sounds like," Charlie said, mumbling around a mouthful of jerky.

"Maybe so," Brandon replied. "But if you choose to fuck around, we'll all be dead. Simple. Got it, Josh?"

"Why Josh?"

"Fuck you, that's why." He hopped down off the table. Emily had vanished. Skeech was still chewing his thumb. "Go get some of that shit of Zooks' for our new friend Josh," Brandon told Skeech, and pulled a cell phone out of his pants pocket. "I gotta make a call."

Brandon left the room and Skeech rose from the couch and started digging through a desk drawer. He put a leather pouch on the desk and unzipped the side, then looked sharply at Charlie. "You talk too much," he said, and grabbed the roll of duct tape off the top of a filing cabinet.

"Please, please don't," Charlie moaned.

"Shut up," Skeech said, and tore off a long strip.

"Please, just a small strip on my mouth, don't wrap it around my head."

Skeech looked at the tape, sighed, and tore it in half, then covered Charlie's mouth. Back at the desk, he removed a syringe from the pouch, filled it from the glass vial, tapped it, then wheeled Charlie over beside the desk chair. He missed the vein three times before he finally found it, and Charlie once again felt the world sag, shudder, and fall away.

CHAPTER 10

He wanted to yell, to shake, to wobble his chair over onto the floor, but Charlie couldn't quite remember how to do any of those things, and besides, he felt better than he had in a long time. In forever. He felt so good that he didn't care when Brandon ran his leg into the door frame as he wheeled him out into the warehouse, so good that he wasn't a bit scared when a polished black SUV appeared, so tired that he nodded off when the doors of the SUV opened and several polished men in black pants and shirts and shoes and sunglasses got out and started talking to Brandon. He woke when one of the men shook his shoulder roughly, tore the duct tape from his mouth, and called over his shoulder, "He's going need a bath."

"Rubber ducky, you're the one...." Charlie sang to himself, woozily.

The man in black stood perfectly still. His hair was tightly clenched and he wore a plug in his ear.

"Keep singing and I will gag you," he said finally. Charlie stopped singing.

The man turned and walked to where Brandon and the other three men in suits stood, talking in low voices. Charlie could only make out stray words: suitcase, Matterhorn, nothing to worry about...He was pretty sure "Matterhorn" was not right, he was hearing things, the sounds were clumpy, his whole life was clumpy, the thought of which made him start to laugh uncontrollably. He was drooling on himself, he knew, but the pure, uncut absurdity of his situation struck him the way a wave could roar up at the beach and knock you down. He probably had bedsores on his ass by now, he thought, which made him laugh even harder. He could feel other bodies gathering around him, but he was laughing too hard to care.

"What's wrong with him?"

"I don't know, he's been like this since we got him."

"Didn't you sedate him?"

"Hell fucking yes we sedated him, he's just off."

A hand slapped Charlie, hard. He stopped laughing and tried to focus.

"Oy, with the slapping and hitting again?" he said, and fell back into convulsions. More hands grabbed his arm and he felt another needle prick in his arm. What had he been laughing at? The gravity in the room shot up and he found could not lift his head, could barely keep his eyelids at half-mast, though he was no longer sleepy.

"What is your name?" Charlie lolled his head and tried to see who had spoken. Everyone in the semi-circle around his chair wore the same kind of pants and shoes, except for Brandon, who wore parachute shorts and beat up sandals..

"Charlie Price." Someone laughed stiffly. Brandon.

"See, he's fucking out of it."

"He'd better be." Several pairs of black pants left the semi-circle. Brandon shifted his weight from foot to foot. The black pants returned.

"What is your name?"

"George W. Bush." Brandon laughed again, more loosely.

"See? See? Look, the photo has him with a beard and a fucking yarn cap or whatever, of course he don't look like that now." Charlie remembered leaving the carnival when he was a kid, walking through a maze of cars parked on the grass, looking back over his shoulder again and again at the lights and music of the midway.

"What is your name?"

Charlie sighed. He heard Emily's voice whisper "Go on," and knew he had only one way out.

"Tebow. Josh Tebow."

Several of the black pant legs shuffled a bit.

"Can you tell us where are you from, Mr. Tebow?"

"Wherever you—" and then he coughed, and began to wretch.

"What did you give him?"

"Pentothol, never mind, shut him down for now." Someone put

a bag over Charlie's head, and he felt yet another needle prick, this time in the left arm, and he fell into something far deeper than sleep.

Charlie drifted for the next few days, or it might have been weeks, or a few hours—he woke once because he was being hosed off on a concrete floor; once in a hospital bed, connected to an arcane rigging of hoses and drips; once seated in front of a bank of hot lights, trying desperately to separate the questions being shouted at him from behind the lights from the questions he heard in his head. He spent a lot of time realizing he was being moved, with a bag over his head and his hands cuffed in his lap. After a while, he just waited for the needle prick to help send him into a small, warm cave where he could sit and bicker with Emily.

"Don't you even care that they're doing this to you? Or even who they are?" This was a common line of inquiry, and he was tired of it.

"No, I give up, I surrender. I don't even know if this is really happening, maybe I'm like the guy in that Roald Dahl short story, the one where he watches the rabbit eat it's babies..."

"This is not like my story, not one bit!" said Georgie, who appeared to Charlie's left. This was becoming a problem: characters from books and movies popped into existence as soon as Charlie thought of them.

"Go away," Charlie said, and Georgie turned to mist.

"Keep that up, I might believe you actually are crazy," Emily said. "Can you do other people? Like, people you just know, not literary characters?"

Charlie thought for a moment, then heard "oh, honey, what is this?"

"Go away, Mom," he said. She went away.

"You always did treat her like crap," Emily offered.

"I know, you're right. But that's not her."

"Well, I'm not me and you're talking to me."

"Yeah, why is that?"

"Unresolved issues?"

Charlie laughed. "Ok, probably, so: I'm sorry. How about that? I'm sorry I was such a callous shit, I'm sorry I treated my mother so bad, I'm sorry I broke Larry Mankowicz's nose in third grade—"

"It was never straight again, you know," Larry said.

"Go away, Larry."

"Ok, let's get on with this, you can't spend your time in some weird K-hole, imagining conversations with imaginary people. Seems to me, you have two choices," Emily said, spinning her chair around to sit with her arms on the back. "You can die, end it, but you'd have to find a way and the very strange people who keep schlepping you around—did you know you're in New Jersey?—have some very clear interest in keeping you alive, too that could be tough. But I have faith in you, Charlie, if that's what you want, you can do it!" She pumped both fists in the air in a mock cheer.

"And the other choice?"

"Live through it. But that means living, no more sitting in a cave. Figure out how to get out of this situation. Figure out what the situation is, first—no, actually, figure out why you want to live, first, then do the rest of it." She tilted back in her chair and smiled, and he remembered once more why he had loved her.

"Ok. Reasons to live." It was very quiet. Water dripped somewhere.

"Oh come on, fuck." Emily stood up and stamped toward the back of the cave. She grabbed one of the walls and drew it back like a curtain. Several figures stood there, frozen, waxy looking, but recognizable: Charlie's Mom, Grady, Beth, Mo, Greg, Derek Cavuto, even Big Al, frozen, but somehow floating.

"This is why I want to live? For Derek Cavuto?"

"Sure, to get him back, right? And your Mom, and Grady, because you owe them, and you love them, and, well, sure, this bitch—" she waved dismissively at Beth, "and Mo and Greg, yes he's a shit but still, think of how your friends would feel if you were just gone. You rip a hole in people's lives when you do that."

"Is that a fact."

"Yes, Charlie, I know that, I know it now, and believe me, I regret it, more than you can know. That's why I'm here."

"Ok—Big Al?"

"Because he's lonely. He really looked forward to bullshitting with you."

"He looked forward to checking out my ass."

"Well, that too, but so what? It's not Al, per se, it's all the people, like Al, that you change when your life comes in contact with theirs."

"Right, it's a wonderful life, I get it. Tell me more about revenge."

"Your choice, now, is to respond to your circumstances in the way that most preserves your humanity, your sense of what 'humanity' means." Charlie shook his head. Emily was gone, and a thin, white haired man in a very nice suit sat opposite him.

"My sense of humanity says to find Derek Cavuto and peel off his skin while his family watches."

"I believe such a response is how you ended up in this situation in the first place."

"It's the American way, bub."

"Viktor."

"Sorry. Viktor."

"So you believe your response should be predicated on your identity as a citizen of the United States?"

Charlie shrugged. "I don't know what to think. I've clearly lost my mind, maybe I just need to turn it off for a while."

"You can't turn it off, I'm afraid."

"No? I'm pretty sure that's what *American Idol* is for?"

Viktor chuckled. "You must first recognize that you are suffering, and then respond to that suffering in the most dignified way you can."

"Dignified? I've pissed myself, ejaculated on myself for God's sake, I'm a drooling mess with a bag over my head, and random people keep sticking me with needles and yelling at me. Where's the dignity in that?"

"Just remember: the angels are lost in perpetual contemplation of an infinite glory...."

"Huh?" Light flooded the cave and Charlie's skull ached the way it had the time he stuck a fork in a socket because his mother told him not to. He was in another room full of lights, but the room was smaller, and as his vision adjusted, the lights were not as harsh as before.

"What is your name?" said a voice behind the lights. The voice was cold, pointed, feminine.

"Josh Turblow. I mean Tebow." Charlie answered. "Can I have some water, please?"

The voice asked Charlie many questions, some of which he'd heard before, some of which were new, none of which did he have an answer for. It asked him about people with Arabic and African sounding names, and when and where Charlie had met them. It asked about his trip to Pakistan. It asked him about high school in West Virginia. Charlie tried to piece together the evidence, all the while answering, truthfully, "I don't know" to every question. Then it fell together: the guy in the freezer, the guy he was pretending to be, was some kind of terrorist, or maybe a spy. Perhaps it was time to start telling the whole truth and nothing but. The lights went off, and Charlie sat in darkness once again. It was very cold, and then the bag was over his head again, and the needle prick in his arm as he tried to get the words out: "Wait, wait, no, my name..."

CHAPTER 11

W.W.W.D.? Charlie snickered. What would Wolverine do, if he woke in a drug-addled stupor with a sack on his head, feeling his ears pop and realizing he was on an airplane? He would break lots of shit, that's for sure, and kill a bunch of henchmen, and then leap from the wreckage of the bad guy's plane to another plane, or maybe to the boss man bad guy and cut him out of his parachute harness and use it himself while the boss man fell and fell. He'd do more than snicker and make up acronyms, that's for sure. Charlie had felt the pull of the cave, heard Emily's voice calling from inside, he didn't even know he could resist it but there, he felt it, the metal, the electricity in his bones, crackling, shunting away the desire to sink into a warm, dark hole—but not like Wolverine, no. No more stupid pop culture shit, though that sounded like a good plot, for a comic book, he could see the panels forming in the darkness around his head. "Hey, you hear me?" That was not the cave, someone was whispering to him, one of those loud, hoarse whispers people used when desperation had almost, but not quite, overcome caution. "Yes, I hear you," Charlie answered.

"Where are they taking us?"

"I have no idea."

"What did you do? I did nothing, I am late at work and in the parking ramp they are suddenly taking me here. What did I do?"

"I don't know what you did," Charlie said, "and I sure the hell don't know what I did."

"Oh they are going to kill me, I know. I will disappear. Can you help me? What is your name?"

This is a trick, Charlie thought. Maybe he wasn't even on a plane, it was all a psychological ploy. "Uh, I'm Josh."

"Josh, I am Khalid. Can you help me?"

"Don't think so, I'm cuffed and have a bag over my head."

"That's enough talking," a new voice said, and Charlie felt something touch his thigh, then felt his brain spasm. His body shook like it was falling down the side of a mountain.

Khalid didn't try to speak again, and neither did Charlie. The drugs were beginning to wear off. Charlie could smell the funk of many unwashed bodies, mixed with the stench of industrial-strength cleaning fluid. Every so often someone let out a sob, or snored. How long had he been here? What day was it? What month was it, for that matter? Maybe he could get his old job back, when they landed he would call Big Al. The plane began to turn, and then to descend, and Charlie cringed and worked his jaw violently, trying to pop his ears. Then they were on the ground, and voices started barking at them in a language Charlie didn't understand. Someone yanked him to standing position by his shoulders and yelled at him in English, "Move it, move it, forward!" He staggered in the direction the hands shoved him.

After two or three stiff-kneed steps, he was turned roughly to the left and felt heat leaking in up ahead, brutal, dry, withering. He bumped into someone standing in front of him and apologized, felt hands shove him again toward the heat. "Stop!" the voice commanded. He stopped. A hand grabbed the back of his neck and shoved his head down, and he nearly melted. "Watch your step," the voice said again, strangely courteous. He felt stairs, took the steps one at a time, carefully, realizing halfway down that he was squeezing his fingers together so tightly they ached. As he reached flat ground another set of hands grabbed his handcuffs and latched something to them, then yanked him forward. Great, now he was on a leash. His skin was peeling off his body and he was leashed and being dragged like a dog. The temptation to simply fall on the ground and refuse to move was strong. Then more hands on his neck, folding him down into a cushioned seat and, ah sweet Jesus, air conditioning. Voices chattered around him in a language he didn't recognize, the cadences fluid and guttural at the same time. Someone turned a key, and they were driving.

Charlie tried to think of some way to keep track of time, to figure out how long they drove so he might have some idea where he was, an idea he knew to be ridiculous, but also necessary for his sanity. Time and space were connected, how far could a car travel in an hour? Or a van, or whatever vehicle they were in, it felt like it was moving at a good clip on a bumpy road, judging by the severity and frequency with which his teeth jarred against each other. Small conversations would crop up around him from time to time, at least four different voices, one behind, one to the left, two in front. Another, silent body slumped in the seat to his right. "And boy does he smell," Emily's voice intruded, and Charlie sent a shock up his spine to blast her out of his head. Her voice tried to speak itself several more times during the course of the journey, and each time he blasted it away, like playing *Duke Nukem*. It was fun.

Leaving the vehicle was much like entering it: hands grabbing and yanking him, voices barking in what he decided must be Arabic, but instead of stairs down, there was a long slope, several short, sharp turns, and then someone kicked him in the small of his back and he fell forward, smacked his head into a wall, and bit his tongue as his fall toward the floor was interrupted by some sort of platform. His mouth was filled with blood, and he felt blood running over his right eyebrow. He got to his knees and found the platform butted against another wall, and that he could sit on it and lean back. His tongue and head throbbed, but the pain was abstract, distant from his body. *What is happening to me? What is going to happen?* These were strange questions, he decided, they meant that somehow he gave a shit what happened, and he felt all the months and years of not giving a shit stretched out behind him, muddy tire tracks leading back to—but what did he care about, now? Survival? Was that all there was, was it that fucking simple? He felt someone standing beside him, and the sack was drawn slowly off his head. "Ouch, that's gotta hurt," a voice said, as Charlie struggled to see.

By the time his vision returned, he was alone again. He wiped blood from his eye with his sleeve, found his wrists still manacled, looked down at his shirt and pants, both a dull green color. They reminded him of hospital scrubs, but heavier, when had they put him in these? He remembered being hosed off. The platform he sat on was a kind of shelf, but padded, bolted to the wall; it was perhaps four feet long, as was the room. He stretched his foot out and touched the far wall, his knee bent, and noticed his feet had been unshackled at some point. The room had a metal door with a small frame at eye height for a window, but no window, and there was a speaker and what looked like a sprinkler head on the ceiling. So. Was the door open? He stood, felt the floor rush up at him, and sat back down. He stood again after a bit and tried to turn and face the door, but the space between the platform and the wall wasn't wide enough, so he shimmied sideways and pushed at the door. Might as well push the fucking wall down, he thought. He lay down on the platform, one foot on the floor, the other propped against the wall, both at ninety degree angles. Comfy. A web of tiny cracks laced a yellow stain on the ceiling.

He woke as the door banged open, letting in hot air and pushing a spike of pain into his forehead. Two men in military dress lifted Charlie off the platform by his arms and pushed him through the door, ignoring his stuttering protests. They guided him down a long hallway, past several doors like the one to Charlie's cell. As they turned a corner, he thought he heard someone sobbing. At the end of that hall was another door, this one wider and painted black. One of the soldiers pushed a button beside the door and it slid open. Charlie noticed he looked very young, judging by the acne on his neck and face. The second soldier gave Charlie another shove, and he went through the doorway. They led him to a metal chair, pushed him down into it, and chained his cuffs to a metal loop on the floor, then retreated. Charlie heard the door slide shut behind him.

His chair faced a long, ragged conference table with three empty folding chairs facing him at the other side. Now we're getting somewhere, he thought, now the trial can start! Bring it on! Muzzy fluorescent lights ticked overhead. His arms and legs ached, his wrists were red and chafed, but he felt almost giddy, surging, ready to... to have an adventure, that's what this was, right? All those times he'd been careful, not stealing from the grocery store, his friends spitting dust from the wheels of their dirt bikes as they sped away and left him, friends no longer, or telling his mother when another group of kids soaked a nerf ball in gas and lit it and kicked it around the parking lot. Even trying to lose his virginity, how many girls did he not try to kiss or even talk to before Sheila Pfaff manhandled him upstairs at a party after prom—Haley Ridenour had been his date, a science nerd, he remembered her as very thin and nervous, she'd asked him, and even brought the corsage. Didn't she get killed shortly thereafter, away at college, a car wreck of some kind, or maybe—the more he tried to remember, the more he saw her face trying to look at him without looking as he came down the stairs after fucking Sheila; she had changed into a sweatshirt and sweatpants and only said "I'm ready to go, if you can take me home," and he did, stopped the car and even tried to kiss her and she laughed, a frightening, animal sound, put a hand on his chest and said "not in a million years," got out of the car and he never saw her again and then she died? Or was he making that part up? Sheila didn't die, she had three kids already, he saw here once in a while at the store or—a door to the left of the conference table opened and three people entered and sat at the folding chairs. Sheila had a nice mouth, he thought, it tasted like cherry coke and rum and lavender.

Two men and a woman sat opposite Charlie. He studied them, looking for details to hold on to, marks to identify them by later, like a detective would do, like Mike Hammer would do. The man in the middle had short, grey hair, fatigues similar to those the soldiers had worn, and was studying the contents of a manila folder. The woman and man on either side both wore dark, featureless suits, white shirts, and no ties; the woman had auburn hair drawn up in a bun and wore a pair of squarish silver glasses, the man wore his hair in a part and scowl on his face, which he directed toward a spot just over Charlie's left shoulder. The light was too dim to make out their features clearly, but the scowl shone through well enough. The man in the middle flipped a few pages back into the folder and began reading: "Joshua Tebow, born September twenty-second, nineteen eighty-two, to John and Beverly Tebow, of Reedsville, West Virginia. Youngest of five children, two brothers, Paul and Lucas, two sisters, Ruth and Sarah. Sarah deceased, 1996," he said, folded a page over at the corner, and continued. "Attended public school through third grade, removed for homeschooling thereafter. Is what I have said correct thus far, Mr. Tebow?"

Charlie smiled at the woman, who had begun poking at some kind of phone or Blackberry, then remembered that he was supposed to be Tebow and the man was speaking to him.

"Oh, yes, yes, sounds just right."

The man looked under his brows at Charlie, then continued reading.

"Member, Church of the Nazarene boys choir. Member, Church of the Nazarene Youth Council. Member, Church of the Nazarene Camping Association. Several other Church affiliated group memberships. Member, Boy Scouts of America, troop ninety-three. Says here you also volunteered at the Shinnston Assisted Living Facility, September 1998 through May 2000. Then you started as a stock boy at a WalMart in Kingwood, is that right?"

"Yes sir, I love me some WalMart." The man to the right scowled harder and began drumming his fingers on the table.

"Uh-huh. You worked there until February of 2002, at which point you gave two weeks notice, and then dropped off the face of the earth."

"Did I?" Charlie replied. "Wow. I guess I had other stuff to do."

The grey-headed man put the folder down and sat back in his chair. "Look, son, this can go two ways. Seems like you were an all-American boy, living a good, patriotic life, then you got confused. It happens. So, you can help us, and make it easy on yourself, but more important, you can make it easy on all the young men and women out there fighting and dying for our country, for your country, Josh."

"I can do that?"

"Yes, you can do that. Now I'm not gonna lie, not gonna tell you your recent actions won't result in repercussions. You will, almost certainly, spend some time in prison. Now, what kind of prison, and for how long, well, that has a lot to do with what you do for us."

"Ok, cool, what do I do? I don't think I'd really like prison. Is it like this place at all?" The woman looked up from her phone and tilted her head. She had a large birthmark to one side of her nose, Charlie saw, or maybe it was a shadow, it was hard to tell.

"Well, good, so, let's start with how you got to Pakistan. We know about your friend Rashid, we know about the 'study group' and the skating rink. We got all of those folks under wraps, don't you worry about that. What we don't know is who contacted you about getting to Pakistan, who helped you with the plane tickets, who got you to the camp, what the camp was all about. Let's start with the tickets: we have a series of emails from a Mr. Sinaga, directing you to purchase a disposable cell phone. Did you meet Mr. Sinaga?"

"Nope, never met him."

"Ok, what happened after you bought the phone?"

"Um, hmm, I don't actually remember." This was fun! This Josh guy sounded like a real case. From Jesus camp to Pakistan, nice, probably wore Luke Skywalker pajamas under his robe, but it was fun pretending to be him, and well, he really didn't know anything, other than what they fed him. Should he tell them the truth? They were clearly Americans, well, the guy in the middle was, the other two still hadn't spoken.

"Let me tell you about the other option, Tebow," said the scowling man.

"Sure, right on schedule," Charlie answered.

"I don't know what that means. In fact, I'm going to let you guess: if you don't man up and start answering our questions, what do you think will happen?"

"Hm, that's a good one. I guess, I guess you'd send me to Gitmo? Or maybe Leavenworth? I'm not sure what I've been charged with, so it's kind of hard to say."

"Wrong answer. Correct answer: we turn you over to people who will extract the information we want from you, and if that doesn't work, we bury your body under a rock in the fucking desert. How does that sound?"

"Sounds like it would suck," Charlie replied.

"Yes, it does, doesn't it," said the woman. Her voice was unexpectedly high pitched and squeaky. "We all make bad choices sometimes, Josh, but you need to remember that even bad choices lead to new opportunities. Let me ask you this: do you love your country? The country that nurtured you and your family?"

Charlie stared at the ceiling. It was the same crappy, white, speckled drop ceiling they have in most every building where people sit at conference tables and ask other people questions. It was too bad these questions weren't more interesting, like: how does one love a country? What is a country? A collection of laws, habits, holidays?

"I'm not sure what you mean."

"Do you love the United States of America?" said scowling man. "It's not a hard question. You are a citizen of the United States, and you have committed treason. You make me fucking sick."

"Tell us about the study group, then," said the man in the middle. "When did you first meet Rashid Al-Amin, aka Rashid Jackson, aka Reginald Curry?"

"Never heard of him, sorry," Charlie answered. The man in the middle bent toward scowling man and whispered something to him while the woman began pecking again at her phone, then they all got up from their chairs and left through the door they'd come in, without another word. Charlie felt triumphant. Do I love America? What kind of question was that? Her remembered having to sign a loyalty oath when Big Al hired him for the security gig, and he had signed "Mick E. Mouse," not that Al ever checked. It sounded like Josh Tebow sure loved America, at least until he gagged on it and went bat shit crazy. Poor bastard. What would it be like to live that way? To pray every day, live at church, never sneaking out to the old mill with the pack of Pall Malls your buddy stole from his Grandma, every decision based on what the hive said was right. That's what my dad's life must have been like, Charlie decided. No wonder he was so wild, did Josh Tebow drop acid and get shouted at by a whole congregation? Not likely, it was just 9/11, the endless replaying of footage of the smoking towers, the sleepy mass hysteria that followed, except that instead of draping himself in flag decals, Josh saw something, glimpsed some truth about the way America works that was so alien it shattered his brain. And then he put it together the way he knew, by finding a cause to believe in, a greater truth to glue the broken bits back together. Too bad he didn't see further: that there was no greater truth, it was all a fucking Ponzi scheme. If he had, maybe he wouldn't be dead in a cooler somewhere, or in pieces in the river, which seemed more likely at this point.

The two soldiers came and escorted Charlie back to his cell. As he tried to arrange himself in some kind of comfortable position, he felt cold air blowing down from the ceiling. Well that's nice, he thought, they turned the air on. Is this part of good cop bad cop? The air continued to blow, and blow, until Charlie started to shiver. Then the music started, unbelievably loud, blasting out of the speaker above him, he even recognized the song, what was it, ha! "Mosh," Eminem's whiny protest song, well that's funny, I guess they have a sense of humor.

The joke soon stopped being funny. Charlie tried to keep count how many times they played the song but lost track sometime after they turned off the air conditioning and switched on the heat. Charlie could feel the beat, the words, the notes in his skull. He passed out and dreamed of his mother, woke and continued to think about her, wondered why she hadn't come to rescue him, pick him up out of the dirt of this awful playground with these awful people—oh I have treated her so badly, I only want her to forgive me, please, Mom, I'm so sorry, I didn't mean it. Why isn't she looking for me? There must be bulletins up, posters with my face on them and a little fringe of phone number tear-offs, she would stick them on telephone poles and in laundromats. You only wanted to help me find truth in the Lord, no, she wasn't religious, need to stay in Josh-mind or they will find out, they will surely kill me then, I have to live, I have to tell my mother I love her, then I have to murder the fucking ice cream man. He passed out again, or maybe the air conditioning was on again, freezing the sweat on his skin, the song became a cloud of microscopic insects, millions of them, buzzing around his head, "I exercise my right to express when I feel it's time," yes, that's it, a switcheroo, back in the cooler, they'd switched him with the other guy, the dead guy who looked just like me, well, a lot like me. Charlie, they switched me for Charlie, he was a traitor, then the heat again, and the song stopped, just the sound of the heat blowing through the vent. He realized he had bitten through his tongue. And the song started again.

Two different soldiers, bearded, brown-skinned men, came and took him the other way from the room with the conference table. They cut off his clothes with scissors and put leg cuffs on him and chained him to a metal chair with no seat. Three more men entered, one clearly in charge, one in hospital scrubs, and one dressed like the soldiers who brought him here. "I'm sorry, I'm so sorry, I'll tell you what you want," he moaned. The man in charge stood and smiled a feral smile at him while the other two made clinking noises behind him. He felt a hand, and a blood pressure gauge was slid around his arm. Another hand slid up under his arm and clamped something to his nipple, and he shrieked. Then one on his testicles, the man in charge nodded, and his body arced in the chair and he saw white. "I did it, I'll tell you all about Rashid and Signora whatever, please, please..." and he, or someone in the room, began to sob.

Sometimes he woke in the chair, other times he woke back in his cell. Other times he woke with the man in scrubs peering down at him, or checking the IV in his arm. They must be feeding him through a tube, he thought, he was never hungry, but was always thirsty. Someone changed the song from "Mosh" to some kind of death metal, he couldn't make it out. How did he know what death metal was? How did he know the title of the other song was "Mosh"? He dreamed, of being lost in a jungle, and of his mother, and of his father, and of churches, and streams of cold water, and of babies with their arms and legs burnt off, blackened stumps. After they changed the song, they brought him to a different room and laid him out on a table. There they shaved his body, and then someone, another kind of soldier, took a long, thin scalpel and made tiny cuts all over his body, under his arms, along his thighs, the tip of his penis, the skin below his chin, tiny little nips, nip, nip, each one blooming slightly red, and when they had finished, they dripped what smelled like vinegar all over him until he passed out again. He said he was thirsty and begged for water so they filled a bowl and put it on the floor and told him to lap it up like a dog. He lapped it up. In his cell, the song was always the same, always maximum volume, the cold air, the hot air, nowhere to unfold his limbs, then yet another room, another table, and they covered his face with a towel and held him down and poured water into his mouth and nose and he tried to will his heart to stop, but it would not, and he tried to remember all the prayers he learned as a child, and he called out for his savior.

He woke again in his cell, and the man in scrubs was beside him, pulling up his eyelids, flashing a penlight into them. "Please, help me..." The man pursed his lips but said nothing, stood up, and pulled the door shut behind him. "Our Father, who art in Heaven," why could he not remember any other prayers, any other scripture, what had they done to him? He said the prayer again and again, matching its rhythms to the song that lived in his cell with him, sang it again and again until he slumped over and slept.

"How are you feeling, Josh?"

He woke back in the conference room, the grey haired man and the scowling man again facing him. The woman was not there, and he felt other people behind him.

"Please, I'm sorry, I understand now, I can tell you whatever you want to know, I'm sorry, I'm sorry..." he sobbed. He felt a hand on his shoulder, and a glass of water appeared. He took it and drank. It tasted like metal and fungus and was the most glorious thing he had ever put in his mouth.

"That's good to hear. Is he in acceptable condition?" the man asked.

"Yes, though he really needs more rest," said a voice behind him, and the man in scrubs stepped around to the table. "The shock to his system—"

"As long as everything is within acceptable parameters, you can go now." The man in scrubs hesitated, thought better of it, and returned to the back of the room.

"Now, where were we. Ah yes, Josh Tebow, born September twenty-second, nineteen eighty-two—"

"Yes, yes, I have sinned, I am ready to take the burden of these sins and make amends, please."

"What a wuss," someone said, and he saw her: Emily, standing to one side of the conference table, blood and bile in a smear down her face and shirt.

"What? No..." he stammered, and he felt the walls begin to slide downward, his chair was falling through space, pulling on him, the whole world being sucked down, down.

"Excuse me?" said the scowling man.

"Tell them, Charlie. You aren't the guy, you're not this Josh person, you're Charlie, a pitiful college dropout who thinks he's smarter than everyone else, but who's not even smart enough to stay out of the way of shit like this. Go ahead, tell them."

So he told them, from the beginning. He could tell they didn't really like the story.

CHAPTER 12

Charlie lay down on the platform in his cell, drew his knees up to his chest, and wondered where the music had gone. It was still hot, but not broiling, there was no blast of heat scorching him from above. If he could manage to stretch his legs, the room would be almost livable. Not that he anticipated living much longer. The warm sense of relief that had washed over him after he spilled his guts quickly ebbed away, leaving a sense of dread in its wake, as though he were inside a huge bell and someone outside, someone with a fresh haircut and cold eyes, was drawing back a hammer, ready to strike and shatter the silence. He pictured his mother opening an official-looking letter and sobbing, falling to the floor and crying because he couldn't leave well enough alone, because he was a goddamn idiot and now she was by herself for good. "I'm sorry," he said, then said it again, and again, until he passed out.

He didn't wake when the door opened, so he wasn't sure if the person standing beside him was real. "Are you real, am I still dreaming?" he said.

"No, you're awake, sit up." Charlie rubbed his eyes and sat up. It was one of the guys in scrubs from the interrogation room, except he wasn't in scrubs now, he wore jeans and a light blue button-down shirt. His eyes stared out from dark, bleary puddles. He threw a roll of fabric down next to Charlie. "Put that on. Hurry up." Charlie unfolded a kind of woolen robe, complete with hood. "Why? What the—"

"Put it on, we'll talk later. Put it on, then follow me and do not, I repeat, do not say a word, do not speak, just follow me and do what I say." With that, he stuck his head out the door and peeked out. Charlie stood, his bones crackling stiffly, and fumbled at the robe, looking for a place to put his arms. "Over your head!" the man hissed, so Charlie pulled the robe over his head. "Follow me, and if we see anyone, do not look at them, look at the ground, only I talk, got it?" Charlie nodded.

The man led Charlie down the hallway and through the room with the conference table. The room was empty, except for a small ceramic clown sitting in the middle of the table. Charlie picked it up. "Put that down! Are you trying to get us killed? Jesus," the man said, and grabbed the clown back from Charlie. He stared at it for a moment, shrugged, and put it back on the table.

They went out the door behind the table and down another series of hallways. At every corner, the man stopped and put out his hand for Charlie to halt before peeking around to the next hall. Finally they reached a grey door marked "fire exit" in English, Arabic, and another language Charlie didn't recognize. "Ok," the man said, stopping at the door, "through this door, to the right, twenty feet or so, is my car. The trunk is unlatched, I need you to get in it."

"Oh, no, I don't want—"

"Shut up, I told you, no talking. When we're past the perimeter, I'll let you ride shotgun, but if you want to live, you get in the trunk." Charlie nodded.

They went out the door and Charlie gasped. The night was dark, the moon a sliver, and the sky overflowing with stars. The man gestured at Charlie to hurry, and he hurried, peeking one more time at the night sky as he folded himself into the trunk. The man closed it gently, and Charlie heard him get in and start the car. They drove a little ways and stopped, and Charlie heard voices, then they were moving again. A few minutes later the ride got choppy and Charlie was tossed around like a popcorn kernel for what seemed a very long time, then the car stopped, and the trunk opened. Once again Charlie saw stars, cascading. "Ok, come around and sit in front."

Charlie did as he was told, and the man started the car and began driving again. They were driving across in a rocky, pitted landscape dotted with scrub, and the road was full of holes. "Where are we?" Charlie asked.

"Southern edge of the Rub Al Khazi, about 60 miles north of Ma'rib."

Charlie looked out the window, then back at the man. "I don't know what that means. What country are we in?" The man glanced at Charlie harshly, then sighed.

"Yemen. We're in northern Yemen, heading west."

"Yemen..." Charlie echoed. "Well, damn. And why, who—what am I doing here, in this car?"

"I'm taking you to meet a friend of mine who works for Reuters. You can tell him your story. You're going to have to walk a bit, I have a bag with water and some food in it for you in back."

"Ok. But why? Who are you?" Charlie looked at him again. He was handsome and craggy, his dark hair slashed with grey, a strong nose, wide set eyes, and he looked like he hadn't slept for more than 10 minutes at any time since the day he was born.

"My name is Michael. Mike. Mike DiStefano. I'm a doctor. Well, a resident, kind of. I—they were going to kill you. I heard Reeves talking about it with Haddad, they were going to kill you. I can't let that happen. I wanted to do something, I wanted to help and this guy came to campus and said I could do my residency with the government, right? Help with the war, all that. My sister worked in the north tower, I just wanted to do something, you know? Then he says it's the CIA, and I thought, sure, what the hell, I volunteered, I don't know what I was thinking, guess I thought I'd be a combination of James Bond and Jonas Salk. And so I've been here for thirteen months. I can't take it anymore, I can't let them kill you, you're an American citizen for God's sake." Charlie saw his knuckles were white on the steering wheel.

"Well, I,—thanks," Charlie said.

"I still have nightmares, my sister looking out the window and then her face melting, a ball of fire, her screaming. But now I have other nightmares, too many, they're starting to crowd out the ones about her. I can't believe I'm nostalgic about nightmares." He shook his head. "Is your name really Charles Price?"

"Charlie, people call me Charlie. Yes, that's my name. I can't figure out how all this happened, how I got here. I mean, I know how, I could diagram it out, but it's still not real, somehow."

"I know what you mean," Michael answered. "It's like I'm watching myself from above, watching myself check vitals in a goddamn dungeon..." his eyes slitted. "Do you know what I do, Charlie?"

"You're a doctor, you said."

"No, a doctor heals people. Oh I fix a broken leg when some yahoo wrecks a jeep, I hand out penicillin, I stitched up a goat the other day. But what I'm here to do is make sure the people on the table don't die, I watch them cut people and attach them to car batteries and waterboard them and pull out their fingernails and I check their vital signs to be sure they don't die, because that's somehow worse than all the other things. I'm not a doctor, I'm a torturer." Charlie shifted in his seat and watched the sand and stone slide by.

"Did you ever—have they killed anyone else?"

"Not an American, not on purpose, not that I know of. You're the first."

Charlie thought about that for a moment. "All because I wasn't who I said I was?"

"That, and because they're all freaking out, Reeves, White, all of them, I can't tell you how many people I have seen come through the facility, seen them cry, beg, admit to anything, and as far as I can tell, we got nothing, not a shred of useful information. I can't keep track anymore, they're just bodies... and then you, an American, the first one I saw. Speaking American English, and then you're not even the guy they thought you were. I just can't take it anymore."

"Wow," Charlie answered. They drove for a while in silence, then rounded a bend fronted on one side by a cliff. Around the bend, Michael eased onto the side of the road. They sat in silence, watching first light creep into the horizon ahead. "So," Charlie said, "they're going to pretty pissed at you, when they find out."

"Probably," Michael said as he reached into the backseat for a duffel bag he then dropped in Charlie's lap. "But they won't figure it out for a little while, and by then, I'll be in Sana'a, and you will have told my friend—Hans van Rijn, that's his name, he writes for Reuters—all about what happened to you. That should be more than enough light, I think. Now, do you see that path off to the right?"

"Yes," Charlie saw a rough path bordered with stones branching off into the dark.

"Follow that path over three hills, at the top of the third is a little hut, goat herders use it, it's the only building there you can't miss it. Wait in there for Hans to come. He should be there just after sunrise. There's water and food in the bag."

"Yes, thanks. Thanks for everything, really, I can't believe, well. You saved me."

"You're not saved yet. Go find Hans, tell him what happened to you. He can help you get to the U.S. consulate too. Or maybe a different consulate would be a better idea."

"But I don't really know exactly what happened. I didn't even know where we were 'till you told me. How long was I in the, the—"

"The prison? Eleven Days. Tell him what happened to you. I'll fill in the rest." Charlie nodded, and held out his hand. Eleven days? Fuck, he thought he'd been there a month at least. Mike reached across Charlie's lap and opened the door.

"It'll be light soon, get a move on." Perhaps if Mike knew he wouldn't make it to Sana'a, that 2 hours from now his car would careen off the road and roll over in a field of qat, that he would only wake for a few moments as the car burned, then he might have shaken Charlie's hand. But he didn't know, and he didn't shake his hand. "Just go," he said, and sped off as soon as Charlie closed the door.

Charlie watched the tail lights vanish over a rise in the road. So, I'm free, he thought, though free in this case means alone in a desert in Yemen. But yes, I am free, follow the path, three hills, hut on the third, talk to Hans. If I were Josh Tebow, I could tell myself God was mad at me, or maybe the story about the guy who had all those terrible things happen to him so he could prove he still loved God no matter what. Job. What a fucked up story. The stars were still spread across the sky, but the first hints of morning had washed out some of their brilliance. Why have I never seen stars like this? I remember camping with Kevin and Rachel and Emily out on that hillside, there were lots of stars in the sky, they were in awe, but that was nothing, the sky was so full it made him start to cry. He realized he was not moving, and forced himself onward, up to the top of the first hill. More hills lay ahead, rising sharply to mountainous crags beyond. It didn't match his idea of what deserts were supposed to look like, no sand in wavy mounds or spires of rock like in the Coyote and Roadrunner cartoons, just hills and rocks and, as he could see in the growing sunlight, brown and orange earth everywhere. At the top of the second hill there was a little pile of stones beside the path, haphazardly dumped there, and he kicked at one with his foot, which caused his too-loose prison slipper to fly off into some scrub. As he bent to retrieve it, he heard a cracking noise, like a tree branch breaking, then heard a high pitched 'ting' and saw one of the stones fly apart. As he squinted and bent closer to look at the split stone, he heard another crack and instinct flooded his body and he ran, off the path, away from the rising sun. His other shoe fell off immediately and he nearly cried out as his feet were torn by the stoney earth but he kept running, away from gunshots and spies and death and toward living, toward angels lost in perpetual contemplation of an infinite glory, and then he stubbed his foot on a very large rock and he did cry out, and hopped on one foot, hopped to the edge of an embankment and fell, rolling, losing his bag, rolling like they did when they were kids on the soft grass behind the school except this was not soft grass, it was dirt and rock and it hurt and then he stopped. It felt like every bone had snapped, like he'd been thrown down in a quarry and then the quarry had been thrown into a volcano. So many stars, he thought, and started to laugh, saw the sky full of scuttering insects, each one tethered to a thread so that they wove the sky itself from their machinations. There is no foot pumping this loom, I could not be Josh Tebow if I wanted to, to suppose there is some God up there, or down here, demanding our praise, our attention—unless this God also likes to torture us, unless that cruel bit of shade we all carry is the image of God in mankind, the need to hurt and delight in hurting, in the cries in others, in their obeisance. If that's the case, then this is surely hell, and so a purely indifferent god is preferable, a blind and insensate god, that is the best we can hope for, it is surely the most we deserve.

CHAPTER 13

The Demon Meridianus, a voice in Charlie's head whispered. Aldous Huxley? Or one of those occult books Emily liked to make fun of. The Demon of Midday. It was in one of the books he'd read, a snatch of it, the story of the demon of the midday sun that tried to tempt serfs to lay down their hoes and lay down their bodies and give up, because it was just too goddamn hot and why bother, the local lord would just come take what he wanted and leave you barely enough to survive. Meridiani? Meridiano? He couldn't remember, and he noticed he was drenched with sweat and his body was a single, dull bruise. He tried to open his eyes but they were crusted shut, and when he lifted his hand to wipe them clean he cried out. The hand still worked, so it probably wasn't broken, and he wiped his eyes clean and opened them to a sun even more roaring than the stars were the night before. Ok, he decided, I'll just lie here. Not the most comfortable place to nap, but moving is worse, so... my god it's so fucking hot. Unbelievably so, he wasn't sure he could get up even if he wanted to, it felt like a great hand was pressing him down against the earth, down into sleep.

Then he was being touched by someone, prodded. He heard voices, mumbling, and then he was being poked again, and someone was yelling at him in Arabic. "Ow!" he yelled, waving his hand in front of his face as though warding off gnats. The mumbling voices in the background all stopped at once, as did the poking. Charlie tried to bend his elbows and prop himself up, but he fell back to the ground and wiped his eyes with his hood. He felt hands in his armpits and then he was sitting up, and his spine was a bolt of fire.

He opened his eyes and the fire entered them too, and he squinted, and in the haze he saw a small crowd of people gathered in front of a dust-shrouded bus.

"I would like..." Charlie's voice sounded as dry and crusted and broken as the rest of him—"to refuse to believe this is happening. This is not happening, you are a mirage."

A bottle of water was thrust in his hand and he drank. "You are English?" someone asked, and Charlie squinted up to see a portly, bearded man wearing a white robe, headdress, and some kind of huge, curved knife thrust in a belt worn around his belly. "I, American, I'm from the US." He wiped his mouth and drank again. The man raised his eyebrows. "American? Ah. Why are you in the dirt at the side of the road?"

"That—that is a very long story," he replied. The man nodded. "You are insured?"

"What? Insured for what?"

"You are bloody, you are insured?"

"Oh, injured, yes, probably, I fell down that hill," he answered, tilting his head in the direction of the embankment. The man raised his eyebrows higher.

"Ok, ok, we have going now, you keep this water and call your friends. Bye bye."

"No, wait! I have no friends, I—I'm not supposed to be here, I was kidnapped." The crowd near the bus began to buzz again when they heard the word "kidnapped."

"Kidnap? Oh, ok, well, we have going now. We send the soldier for you, they help you."

"No, no, please don't leave me here," Charlie begged, and tried to rise to his feet. The world spun off its axis and he plopped back down. "Mister Al-Masedi, may we speak with you?" A tall, blonde, very tan man emerged from the crowd and spoke to the man with the knife, who turned and went back to the crowd. Charlie couldn't make out what they were saying, and a young man dressed similarly to the man with the knife came from behind Charlie and squatted beside him, grinning. His cheek bulged, and he spit and grinned and spit again. The older man returned from the crowd and gestured to the young man to get up. "Ok, you come on the Blessed, we take you back to Sana'a with us. But four days, and you have money?"

"No, I have no money. I can get some, later? ATM?" Charlie guessed.

The man sighed and gestured for the young man to help Charlie up, which he did, roughly, but then held on to him while he got his legs and kept hold of him as they walked slowly toward the bus. The crowd, Charlie saw, was comprised largely of Asian men and women, with a smaller group of Nordic-looking folks as well, and their level of chatter grew as he inched his way toward the bus. They parted for Charlie, smiling and nodding and whispering. The young man helped Charlie up the stairs of the bus and led him to the back. Charlie sat and drank some more water as members of the crowd slowly boarded the bus. The tall blonde man was first on, and he came to the back and sat beside Charlie and smiled at him. Charlie tried smiling back, but he was pretty sure it looked more like a grimace.

"Are you hungry?" the man asked, his English betraying only a slight accent. Charlie nodded, and the bus door closed and they started to move. "Ok everyone, welcome back on board the Blessed, our ship of Yemeni desert. We have an added value, as you see, a new passenger, everyone make him feel nice and welcome." The seated passengers erupted into applause, and the blonde man returned to sit beside Charlie. He carried a small knapsack, and took out three energy bars and handed them to Charlie, who tore at them greedily.

"They clap because you are the most interesting thing that has happened on the tour so far," the man said. "I think many of them believe you are an actor, hired by Al-Masedi and planted here. Are you an actor?"

"No, not an actor," Charlie said, spitting bits of power bar as he spoke.

"No, you do not seem like that, the blood is real, yes? You were really kidnapped?"

"Yes, I was kidnapped, and then someone helped me escape, and I fell down the hill."

"Do you know—oh I am sorry, my name is Konrad, I don't mean to be rude." Konrad extended his hand. Charlie shook it gingerly. "I'm Charlie, thanks for the food, I haven't eaten in a while. I had a bag with food and water but I dropped it when I fell down the embankment there."

"Did you not see the hill? It is not a small thing."

"It was dark, and I was running."

"Ah, running, your kidnappers were chasing you?"

"No, someone was shooting at me. I don't know who."

Konrad beamed. "Well, you live a very interesting life, Charlie."

Charlie stopped chewing. Did he know? Was he from the facility? CIA? Maybe he worked for that orange fucker in Pearson. No, stop it Charlie, come on, he thought, you're just around normal people for he first time in quite a while. He nodded and resumed chewing.

"Many of the people here, myself included, also would like to be kidnapped. Without being shot at, of course!" He chuckled and crossed his legs. Charlie swallowed more than he was ready for and coughed. Konrad obligingly slapped him on the back.

"I'm sorry, but do you know what you're saying? Why would you ever want to be kidnapped?"

"Because it's exciting," said a voice, and a woman with a kind face and skin nearly as tan as Konrad's popped up from behind the seat to Charlie's left.

"No, it's really not, not in my experience."

"Well," she continued, "what company did you use?"

"What company?"

"Yes, which tour company?"

"I'm not sure what you're talking about, I was kidnapped," Charlie said, color rising in his face.

"Well maybe that is the problem, you need a reputable company to make the experience exciting. I am Marta, pleased to meet you," she said, extending her hand over the seat. Charlie shook it, looked at Konrad, who nodded, then back to Marta.

"Are you saying that you pay someone, these guys," he gestured toward the front of the bus," to kidnap you?"

"Well, no, not exactly," Konrad replied. "The kidnapping is a bonus, no one can ensure that we are kidnapped, it only comes if we are lucky."

Charlie shook his head and stared down at his filthy hands. "That is, if you don't mind my saying, really weird."

"Why weird?" Marta said. "Most tours are too boring. This one is ok, very hot, some things to look at yes, very old ruins, interesting architecture, but to make it a special time, we may be kidnapped. I don't think I want to be kidnapped like you, though," she said, and rummaged through her knapsack to offer Charlie a fist full of moist towelettes.

"Yes, you look terrible," Konrad agreed.

"Yes, well, I've been—" he couldn't bring himself to say "kidnapped" again—"uh, I've had a tough time the last few days."

"Well," Konrad said, "take some rest, we will be in Ma'rib in a few hours, you can get washed up there. And I promise to wake you if we are kidnapped!" he chuckled again, then got up and sat across from Marta.

"That, that would be just fine, thanks." Charlie smiled weakly at Marta and stretched out on the seat, It was cool, the bus was air conditioned, he could fully extend his legs, and he was not laying in the desert. He was surrounded by lunatics, but that was, he realized, simply the way things were, everyone everywhere was absolutely insane and there was nothing be could do about it except smile and accept their moist towelettes and power bars with gratitude.

Mr. Al-Masedi woke Charlie as they arrived in Ma'rib. He spoke gently, and offered to let Charlie sleep on the bus since he had no money, but Konrad wouldn't hear of it, and so Charlie found himself with a room at the Hotel Bilquis, soaking in a very small, very tepid, and wholly wonderful bathtub. He found three gashes of various lengths from his fall, none of which looked like they needed stitches, and watched the water slowly turn black. After drying himself and dressing he joined Konrad and Marta in their room for a meal of rice and flatbread and some kind of stew, during the course of which every other tour passenger managed to drop by and stare at him: 7 couples from Korea, 2 men and a woman from Holland, another married couple from Germany, and Mr. Al-Masedi and his son, Saeed. Several of the Koreans and all the Europeans all spoke English and inquired about his welfare, and Song, one of the Korean women, volunteered that she was a nurse and cleaned and bandaged his cuts with gauze supplied by the hotel's owner. No one asked why he had been lying on the side of the road, let alone why he'd been kidnapped, though it was common knowledge at this point, and most of them were desperate to know more. But Charlie was traveling with Konrad and Marta now, they had become a unit, as travelers often do, and the rest of the passengers respected their separateness, a respect which did not, of course, preclude the invention of many wild rumors concerning this strange young man and the condition in which he'd entered their lives.

He also discovered, while lounging in his new friend's room, that the date was September 29th, his birthday. He was sure his face dropped after they told him, but he didn't mention the day's significance. Instead, he told Konrad and Marta an abridged version of his story. He left out the part where he threw shit and also the bit about setting Cavuto's car on fire, and amplified the scenes that involved gangsters, the CIA, and his escape. Later he wondered if he'd overdone the ending, but Konrad and Marta were drinking in every detail, and so he told them that he and Michael had to shoot their way out of the facility, fleeing across the desert with a truck full of elite soldiers chasing them through the night. If they were skeptical, they didn't betray any doubt, and left him at the door to his room with praise for his cleverness and fortitude, and with a pair of Konrad's old sandals. As soon as the door was shut, he started to cry, could it really only be a month since he was drinking crappy coffee with Beth outside the gas station? Was it really his birthday, for God's sake? And then he imagined his mother, how the guilt must be eating her, making her drink too much shitty wine, or maybe she's just in shock: your only child disappears from the face of the earth, he couldn't comprehend how that must feel. Or maybe he could, just a little, and he cried harder, and tried to tell himself Mike Hammer wouldn't cry in his bed in a filthy hotel, he would take action, he was alive, Wolverine was a pussy, and then he woke to a knock on the door and Konrad and Marta were there, ready to join him for breakfast.

The bathroom mirror was small and glazed with a yellow grime, but it was enough for Charlie to wonder at the face looking back at him: gaunt, with gashes above his left eye and on his cheek, a field of stubble shadowing his chin—when did they shave him? He had no memory of being shaved, and shivered at the thought of what else they might have done to him—and his eyes were lighter than he remembered, much lighter, washed out and very, very tired. "I am Josh," a voice whispered, NO, he shouted in his head, the angels are lost in perpetual contemplation of an infinite glory and you shut up too, he yelled in his head again and again until the words dissolved and he was panting over the sink, looking anywhere but the mirror.

He dressed and found Konrad and Marta and after eating and whispering to one another about the state of the rest rooms, they joined the tour group headed for the to the ruins of old Ma'rib, along with a truck and two cars' worth of police escorts. The men and their guns made Charlie nervous, of course, but Al-Masedi assured him that they were under the command of one of his cousins, and that they might even help Charlie acquire the proper travel permits, as long as he had his passport handy. When they arrived at the site, Konrad took Al-Masedi aside, and Charlie stayed on the bus, dozing. He woke and looked out the windows at the alien landscape, stripes of red and orange, green valley walls shooting up in the distance, a sky whose color seemed alien, and then he fell back to sleep.

A few hours later, before the rest of the tour returned, Al-Masedi and Konrad came to talk with Charlie. "You have no papers, very bad" Al-Masedi kept repeating, and Konrad kept replying that once they got back to Sana'a, Charlie could go to the consulate and explain what had happened. Charlie reminded Konrad that the US consulate might not be the best place, that there would surely be CIA there looking for him, which sent Al-Masedi off the bus entirely, talking fast into a large cell phone.

"He didn't like the sound of that," Konrad said.

"I'm sorry, I'm just a little paranoid."

"Paranoid? Ah, nervous, yes, that is understandable. If you are too nervous we can go to the Deutsche consulate and request asylum, I am sure they would be very interested to hear your story as well."

"If you think that's a good idea, I'm out of ideas myself," Charlie agreed. The rest of the tour group began to board the bus, peeking at Charlie and talking nervously. Word had spread quickly, and he was no longer a novelty, but a potential threat.

The road to Sana'a was better paved, and the smoothness of the ride, combined with the air conditioning, made the passengers drowsy, save Al-Masedi, who continued have what sounded like nine different conversations at once on his phone. His voice became like a fly buzzing on a hot summer day, and then stopped. The sun had just started setting, and some of the passengers began snoring earnestly as the bus drifted to a stop. Charlie looked out the window and saw a figure on a camel ride by, holding a gun with one hand and a set of reins in the other. The passengers roused, then started buzzing and bobbing up and down in their seats like prairie dogs. Charlie shrunk lower in his seat as Konrad rose and started walking down the aisle. "All to please remain in your seats," came Al-Masedi's voice over the loudspeaker, and Konrad obliged. Three decades from now, recently widowed and soaking in a spa in Oberstaufen, he would hear the same voice, the same message, over the public address system, inspiring him to sell his fertilizer business and devote all his time to researching human memory and cognition, but now he only sat down beside Charlie and frowned, his hand on Marta's knee, the same knee that would give way three decades hence and cause Marta to slip from the curb and crack her head on the pavement.

Al-Masedi disappeared down into the door well, allowing a man wearing a dusty white robe and checkered head scarf to board the bus, gingerly carrying a small machine gun with the tips of his fingers. He marched down the aisle, glaring left and right at every set of seats, stopping at the end to stare at Charlie. He was handsome, even beautiful, with a neatly trimmed beard, large green eyes, and the sort of nose that graced ancient coins. Charlie felt himself shrinking further into the seat, trying to slide into a seam of the cushions. The man nodded, turned, and walked briskly off the bus, after which Al-Masedi reappeared and fumbled loudly with the microphone. "Ladies and gentleman, I am required to inform that we on the bus are asked to accompany the men outside to their home, where you will be given food and a place to rest. Thank you." With that, he disappeared again, and the bus began slowly to roll forward. The passengers twittered excitedly. "A kidnap! Thank you, Charlie," Marta said.

"What? I don't have anything to do with it," he replied.

"Oh, I think you do," Konrad interjected. "Not intentionally, of course, but I think you are the lure that brought the fish!"

"Shit shit shit…" Charlie muttered under his breath. Why was this happening to him? His bones were not electric, he had no Betsy in his pocket to blast the bad guys, he didn't even know who the bad guys were. He peeked out the window as the bus picked up speed: he saw no people, no one riding horses or camels or anything else, just mountains and yellow earth and clouds listing above. Konrad and Marta tried chatting with him, but he only grunted—they were excited, this was somehow an important part of their vacation, getting kidnapped. It's not fun, he wanted to tell them, and if this is the kind of thing that excites you then, well, you are fucked in the head, but he couldn't say it, he just looked out the window and thought about his father, hallucinating, tied to a tree while his people tried to shout the devil out of him.

The bus turned off onto a dirt road, then stopped. The tour group was led off the bus and up a short, steep slope to large compound of brown and white and orange earthen buildings, many of them several stories high. There were goats and chickens in the street, and when one of the Koreans tried to snap a picture of them his camera was taken, gently but at gunpoint, by one of the men who had led them up the hill. They were then herded to a large courtyard in the center of the compound where the man who had first boarded the bus stood, apparently waiting for them. Charlie noticed several old men sitting against the wall, their cheeks bulging grotesquely on one side, like bifurcated Dizzy Gillespies. Their knees hovered in front of them, tied by some kind of strap, and each had a large knife in his belt, like Al-Masedi had, like the men who'd led them up the hill had, like just about everyone had, he thought. While the tour group stared at the man in charge, he stared back at them; he seemed to be counting, Charlie thought. Then he began to talk, surprisingly, in gently accented English:

"Greetings, welcome to my home and the home of my family. I hope your homes and families are safe and prosperous. My name is Marwan Jam'an Yaslim Al-Attah, and I am speaking with you as a member of the clan of Hashid, of the Banu Hamdan confederation. I am very sorry to have interrupted your sightseeing. We request your presence as our guests until which time certain requests we have made of the government of Yemen are granted us. I trust your stay here will not be long, if Allah wills it. We have prepared separate quarters for men and women, please accept my apologies if you are a married couple, for us, this is the best way. Please follow Akrad," he said, gesturing to a man standing slightly behind him," if you are male. If you are female, please follow the path to the right where Nadeen is waiting to take you to your quarters. Again, please accept my humble apologies, I hope our hospitality will remove some of the sting from this discomforting situation."

Charlie fumbled into the back of the group of men as the English speakers among them translated for those who did not. The air was hot and dry and dusty, and he realized he was not uncomfortable, he even liked it, liked climbing the rocky hill and sweating lightly, liked the wispy clouds barely standing out from the rest of the sky. The men formed a line with the help of some of their kidnappers and started walking around the side of the building, with Charlie in the rear, just behind Konrad. "Isn't this exciting!" Konrad whispered over his shoulder. Charlie wasn't sure it was exciting, but so far it was much better than being drugged and gagged and hooded. A hand grasped his elbow lightly and Manwar's voice followed, in a register far lower than the declamatory rumble he'd used a few seconds prior, but with no less authority: "but not you."

CHAPTER 14

Charlie wondered if anything would ever surprise him again. Manwar led him into the central building, through heavy, intricately carved wooden doors set in walls of whitewashed clay, flanked at either side with recessed windows that reminded Charlie of the sunken eyes of Josh, the dead man in the cooler. He flinched, and all he knew about his failed double flooded back—do these people think I'm Josh Tebow too? The room they entered was spacious and covered with a patchwork of heavy rugs, the light from the windows muted and dense. A row of men sat along one wall, each sitting with their right knee raised, some with their right arm perched across the knee, some holding the tubes of an enormous hookah. Manwar stopped to slip off his sandals, gesturing with his chin for Charlie to do the same with own, then took Charlie by the arm again and led him to the furthest corner of the room. The men's eyes followed him in unison, and he saw that all of them had the same distended cheek as the men outside against the wall. Manwar sat and waved his hand beside for Charlie to join him. They sat quietly and one of the men set the tube of the hookah down on a little wooden cradle next to Charlie's knee.

"It is only tobacco, and some perfumes, and some spice, you don't need to worry," Manwar said.

"Ok," Charlie said as he lifted the tube and inhaled. It was indeed perfumed, and very spicy, and Charlie coughed until his eyes hurt as the men along the wall laughed mightily.

Manwar let loose a rapid stream of Arabic and one of the men near the end of the row got to his feet and left the room through a small door on the opposite wall. He returned quickly with a wooden bowl and jug and placed them in front of Charlie, grinning.

"Water, pour it in the bowl and drink, if you are thirsty."

"Yes, thanks," Charlie said, and did. The water was warm and tasted of roses.

They sat quietly for a while. Manwar held his head low and gently rocked back and forth.

"What are these windows made of?" Charlie asked.

Manwar turned his head slowly and looked at Charlie as though he'd just crawled out of a septic tank and asked for a kiss.

"What is your name?"

"Charlie. Charlie Price." And I can survive anything, so keep your snotty looks to yourself, he thought.

"Yes. That means nothing to me. Al-Masedi has told us a very curious story about you. We don't often find rogue Americans lying in the dust at the side of the road. You must be a gift from Allah, his will be praised."

"Well, I, I'm not sure what to say. I didn't wake up one day and decide to come here."

"No? So you are not CIA? Not NSA? Blackwater, perhaps?" He poured some of the water into the bowl and sipped.

"Nope, though I was a security guard back home," Charlie answered, chuckling to himself.

"A security guard? Where?"

"Um, an old factory, not much there."

"No, I mean in what part of the United States were you a security guard?"

"Oh, sorry, in Pearson, Pennsylvania."

"Mmm, Pennsylvania, I have not been there."

"You've been to America, though? I mean, your English is great, better than the German guy."

"What German guy?"

"On the tour bus."

"Ah. Yes, I lived in Dearborn, Michigan for nine years, then I attended college at the University of Michigan, also in Dearborn. I visited New York City, and also Minneapolis, and Toronto, though of course that is not in the United States."

"Really?" Charlie sucked on the hookah tube, which had appeared at his knee once again, this time without coughing.

"Really. I studied Political Science, and I played trumpet for the marching band. I was an alternate, so I only got to appear in one game, though we did defeat UCLA handily, 38 points to 9."

Charlie stared. "Seriously?"

"Yes, I received my degree in 1998. The windows are made of stone, actually, a kind of obsidian that craftsmen cut very thin and then polish."

"What? Oh, the windows. Wait, why did you go to Michigan?"

"To the school or the state?" He began scratching the bottom of his foot.

"I don't know, both, this is weird."

"Weird? Not really. I have cousins in Dearborn, most of Yemen has cousins in Dearborn, and as the eldest son, I left when I was nine and went to earn money and go to college. I told my father I was studying engineering, he would not have understood why I wanted to study political science. When he died, I came home to help my family."

"Oh, I'm sorry, that he died I mean." Charlie shook his head and waved off the hookah tube.

"No need, he was, in most every way, a very hard man, hard to know, hard to live with. I did not like coming home to visit because of him He fell into a well three days after my graduation ceremony. So if you are not CIA, NSA, Blackwater, or some other species of mercenary, why did Al-Masedi find you at the side of the road, no passport, no travel certificates?"

Charlie's foot was falling asleep so he shifted it forward and rubbed his thigh. "Do you want the short version or the long version?"

"The short version, first."

"It was a mix-up. I look like another man, I didn't even know the guy, and so I was kidnapped and flown to a prison somewhere near here, I don't know where it is exactly, but the people who ran it were American, and they were going to kill me, and then this doctor helped me escape, but I got lost and fell down a hill and knocked myself out."

Manwar sat quietly for several minutes before speaking again. Charlie saw that most of the other men were dozing "Why were they going to kill you?"

"Because they thought I was the other guy, so I pretended I was, then I changed my mind and told them the truth. The doctor said they were going to kill me, anyway. I believed him"

"Why did you lie? Why did you not just tell them when they first apprehended you that they had the wrong man?"

"I'm not really sure. I was scared, and it was just so easy to pretend, I couldn't believe I was getting away with it."

"It seems like a very poor decision on your part."

"Yeah, I've been making lots of bad decisions lately, I think."

Manwar found something interesting on his foot and beckoned for one of the men sitting beside them. He spoke to him quickly in Arabic and the man disappeared through the same door on the wall as before, returning this time with a long, narrow knife. Charlie flinched, then watched as Manwar started digging into the skin of his heel with the tip of his knife.

"I was Poli-sci, too. In college."

Manwar continued digging for a moment, then stopped and smiled at Charlie.

"Really? Where did you study?"

"At Pearson College, you probably never heard of it."

"No," Manwar answered, then went back to his foot. After a while, he seemed satisfied, and poured a bit of the water from the jug over his heel. Three of the seated men suddenly rose and went out the front door, leaving Manwar and two others, both of whom snored lightly.

"It will be time to eat soon. You are hungry?"

"Yes, thanks," Charlie said. "So why did you kidnap us? The tour, I mean?"

"Because we are trying to build a school. Or rather, we are trying to get our government to build us a school. Saleh is not of our tribe, so we must coerce him to give us materials and workers to build it."

"Saleh is—?"

"The leader of Yemen, the President." Manwar stood and went to the window and stretched, then turned to face Charlie. "I'm sure this seems a strange way to do things, but we are not really a country, only in name, and the man who holds the name and his tribe get everything, unless we force them to give us what we need. This 'kidnapping', as you call it, is very common here in the north. In the south the like to think they are more sophisticated, and that we in the north are crude bumpkins. They will soon learn otherwise."

"Oh. Ok."

"What did you learn about the science of politics in college, Ch—"

"Charlie."

"Charlie. What did they teach you about revolutions, about power, about democracy, about all the many isms men use to enslave other men?"

"Well, lots of things, what do you mean, specifically?"

Manwar sat again. "My people are tribal, traditional, they have survived this way for thousands of years. The south pretended they were Communist for a time, they followed the fools in Egypt and gave a cabal of schoolboys the reins of government. Now we have one country, and they pretend to be a Democracy. Which path should we take? Democracy? Dictatorship? Feudalism?"

"I think—"

"I will tell you," Manwar continued. "We must have an new revolution here in Yemen. We are not going to swallow your Democracy at the end of a gun, the kind you Americans try to foist on everyone. Corporate Democracy, the war on terror, what madness—have you been to Iraq, Charlie?"

"No, never."

"I have been there. Your Democracy is rape, nothing less. The same as our leader rapes the people here, and you help him by giving him money, giving him weapons. No more Democracy. A new Socialist revolution is what Yemen requires. A human revolution." He blew loudly through his nose, a snort in reverse.

"Uh, well, I don't know about what Yemen needs, really, but I totally agree with you about the Democracy thing, America isn't really a Democracy, Bush and Cheney and those crooks are just corporate fronts, I know that's true. Maybe we need a revolution in the U.S. too."

Manwar smiled. "Yes, maybe you do." The main doors swung open and men bearing trays of food swept into the room. The smell of all the different dishes made Charlie slightly dizzy. He was handed a wooden plate, which he started piling with food. "Eat as much as you like, please, you are my guest while you are here." Charlie looked for a fork and noticed the other men eating with their hands, so he used a clump of rice to scoop some vegetable melange into his mouth. It tasted so good he nearly cried.

"So what will happen to me once you get your school?" He asked.

"We do not talk at dinner. Eat, then talk. Here," Manwar handed Charlie a thick napkin. "Right hand only."

Charlie couldn't remember ever eating so much, his stomach was bloated, his head lolled on his neck like an overripe fruit. He leaned back against the wall and fought sleep. Just as sleep was winning, Manwar stood abruptly and tapped his shoulder. "Come," he said, and Charlie reluctantly followed. He lead Charlie through the moon-lit courtyard to a small opening in the wall, ducked his head, and went through. "There," he pointed at several small huts at the top of a ridge, "is the bathroom. There is water there to wash with, and towels. Do not put the towels in the hole, put them in the basket beside the hole."

He was waiting when Charlie emerged from the hut. "Tell me," he said, walking up along the ridge, "what sort of revolution America should have."

"Well, I'm not exactly sure, but the way things are going now are just, uh, unacceptable, rich bastards get everything, poor bastards watch their kids go to war so everyone can drive SUVs. It's messed up."

"But you are a rich country, even your poor are rich."

"I guess, compared to, well, here—" He looked for a reaction, but Manwar kept walking, head bowed slightly.

"Yes, well. What we need here is, like you think America needs, is more equality. Here we also have the yoke of orthodoxy. I am a good Muslim, blessed be his name, but too many of our religious leaders are backwards, and interested only in preserving their own power. My Uncle, for instance, the Imam of our village, is very backward, very foolish. If we are to have revolution in Yemen, it must be a human revolution, such as Rosa Luxemborg proposed. Do you know Rosa Luxemborg?"

"No, ah... nope."

"She was a great revolutionary, she recognized that the people needed freedom and joy, they needed to be able to laugh and dance and feast as well as work. Tonight, we will go to a dance in the courtyard, and the women will peek from the window's of the women's quarters while the men stand about and wish they had women to dance with. The Imam will come after an hour or so and disperse the dance, and then will publicly chastise me. The same thing has happened three times now. It is hard to teach revolution when old men look over your shoulder."

"That's really brave of you. It's dangerous, right? Is there no dancing in Yemen?"

"Ha, it is not so brave, we have the dance for our guests, my family will not dance, though the children might. If it were not for the guests, there would be no dance."

"I know what you mean about religion, or, well, no, I don't really know at all, but there are fundamentalists in the US too."

Manwar stopped and looked at Charlie. "Do the fundamentalists run your country?"

"No, not quite, but they are pretty powerful."

"They are powerful here too, but the people want to be free. I know they do, even if they don't know it yet."

The dance was not quite what Charlie expected: an ancient boom box playing what he guessed was Yemeni pop music, well-abused folding chairs for the tour group, men on one side, women on the other, and jugs of rose water. The local men, half a dozen of them, shepherded young children in to the center of the courtyard, spitting from their distended cheeks. Soon enough, the children started to dance, and Manwar addressed the crowd, telling them they would only be required to stay for a few days, and to please accept his hospitality and enjoy themselves. Various couples began finding each other, whispering excitedly as they met on the 'dance floor'. Some sat together and talked, a few snatched quick kisses and looked to see if anyone had spotted them. Konrad came to speak with Charlie, but Manwar held his palms outward and stood between them, blocking the way. "No, please, you are not to speak with him."

"It's ok, he's a friend," Charlie said.

"No. You are a special case, you are not part of the this group," he answered. Konrad looked back over his shoulder, eyes narrowing.

"Special case, huh? So what does that mean, exactly?"

"We can discuss this later. Come, I will show you where you can sleep."

Manwar led Charlie to a small room in the central building. Two other men already slept there, thickening the air, but Charlie found the rug he lay upon remarkably comfortable, and he fell quickly asleep. He woke in the middle of the night and saw the moonlight surging through the stone windows. One of the men snored loudly, the other made small whimpering noises and ground his teeth. Charlie decided to count all the things he'd done in his life that he wasn't proud of: Emily, of course, the way he'd handled that whole thing; yelling at his mother when he found her and Eddie, one of her boyfriends, sleeping off a drunk, naked, in the tent he kept in the backyard the summer before he went into sixth grade; cheating on his Biology final in High School, and his Algebra final, and those papers he bought in college; throwing shit at Derek Cavuto, that was not a classy move; Haley Ridenour and the prom... I've not been so nice to women, but then I never really had many guy friends, or many friends at all—oh, there was stealing a lump of hash from Greg's desk that time, but now that he knew what he knew about Greg, it didn't feel so wrong. The snoring man let out a shout and sat up, shook his head, glanced over at Charlie and the other man, then lay back down and was quickly snoring again. A millipede the size of a squirrel shot across the wall, and Charlie found himself wondering if any of his life had been worth living at all.

CHAPTER 15

The next three days were among the most restful of Charlie's life. He wandered about the courtyard, played with the seemingly endless stream of children that swelled down from the hilltop where they had their open-air school, ate plentifully, though the dried camel jerky was a bit much for his stomach, and took long walks through the hills with Manwar and his cousins Yasser and Na'em, neither of whom spoke English, but were fond of playing jokes on Charlie, like giving him a chunk of camel jerky and watching his reaction. They both also chewed prodigious amounts of qat, which Charlie soon learned was the bane of Manwar's existence: "All day, my family, the men of my whole family, the family of Yemen, the chew and chew and talk and forget to work, forget that they are starving and exploited. I tell them no, that we will soon run out of water because we use it all for qat, but they just smile, it has burrowed its way deep into our men and will kill us all."

"Only men? Or do you mean men like everyone, what is that called?"

"It is gender-specific, not 'presume not God to scan, the proper study of mankind is man,' but men, the male gender. Women do not, ah, most women do not chew qat. Some few do, I have not met one but I have heard of them. Perhaps that is they key, I must teach the women and let them teach the men, even as I teach the men as well..."

"What did you say? About presume not God...'?"

"Ben Jonson, I believe, one of your poets. I loved to read many of your poets, many of your authors, your novelists, it is important work for a revolutionary to know people, to know their hearts. Tell me about your people, what kind of people live in Pablum?"

"Pearson," Charlie replied, and Manwar nodded. "The usual American people, I guess. But then, I took a road trip to New York City once, and the people there pretty different from the people in Pearson, or even Pittsburgh. And I've been a few other places, all in the Eastern part of the US, and yeah, the people were kind of different, but the same stuff was everywhere, McDonalds and Pizza Hut and WalMart and, stuff like that."

"And I ask about your people and you tell me about American stores? I know American stores, I worked in my Uncle's shop for 7 years, after school and summers and breaks in college. What are your people like, Charlie?"

Charlie stopped and looked at the scabby green and yellow hilltops rolling away from him, lowering to plain in one direction, rising to mountains in the other. "My mother is my only real people, I guess. My family, I mean. Some of her boyfriends were ok, and I had a bunch of people I knew from the neighborhood and from school, but I don't think I have people the way you mean it."

"Alright, then what of the American people? Not their stores, but why they hate Muslims, why they think the planes that struck the trade center were the force of all Muslims hating them, or why they treat their women so shamelessly, or why their women agree to it. Or why do you go to war so quickly, why do you invade Iraq, why do you believe the lies of Bush when it is clear to anyone that the planes that struck your trade center were Saudis," and Manwar spat, as he always did when mentioning Saudis.

"Which question do you want me to answer?"

Manwar laughed. "I'm sorry, just tell me about the American people. In your estimation."

"I think most Americans are fat, lazy, and hopelessly ignorant, and they like it that way," Charlie said. "But then I know plenty of good people who tried to stop the war, the wars, whatever, I went and marched in Pittsburgh with my girlfriend..." Charlie saw Emily dart behind a bush and slowed to a stop.

"Ah, you have a girlfriend? Or a wife, now?"

"No, not anymore."

"I'm sorry. I have two wives, both chosen to strengthen allegiances with our neighbors. I try to teach them, but only Naseem will listen, and she only does so to please me. I will tell you what I think of American people. Yours is a nation founded on the principles of the Enlightenment, of rational thought and expertise and knowledge, of a world that is explainable, made by a God who is not. But your nation was founded because of a revolution, which is a Romantic idea, a challenge to rationality, to the idea of expertise and authority and knowledge that is power. So you are founded by a contradiction, I mean a contradictory impulse, and so you are fractured from the beginning, always being pulled apart but always being pulled back together. Once I understood this, I understood America, all the things I saw while I was there."

"Are you reciting your senior thesis to me?" Charlie asked.

"Ha, no," Manwar laughed, "only the outline of an argument I had with my thesis advisor for many months. She believed more in the waves of immigrant groups shaping and reshaping American identity. She was also very pretty. Much prettier than you."

"Ah, must have been distracting."

"I come from a country where women are still not allowed to ride in cars with men they're not related to. The distraction of women who are present in the world began as soon as I arrived, when my female cousin picked us up at the airport. It was the first thing I saw in my life that really made me think."

Three days of conversations such as this inspired Charlie to try and list all the books he had read during his time as a security guard, especially when he found out Manwar had read both *Anna Karenina* ("Count Vronsky was a piggish man, I did not understand him, or what Anna saw in him") and *Invisible Man* (the work of a true revolutionary!). He didn't recognize a lot of the references Manwar made, but when they talked about political history, he could feel names and concepts flaring in his head, things he knew and had studied and cared about at one time, or at least pretended to care about, he didn't know which it was, who he was then. He first tried to make another list, with the waxy paper and thick pencils Manwar had provided him, of all the political ideas they discussed, all the ideologies and thinkers, but he could barely recall them once he was back in his room. He remembered only the shape of their conversation, and Manwar's radiant conviction, and the sense that he was somehow helping Charlie put himself back together.

The tour group left on the third day in a cluster of military transports manned by bored, moustached soldiers. In days prior, Charlie had seen Konrad a few times in the courtyard, raising his eyebrows at him, waving, but Charlie was not part of the tour anymore, he'd never really been part of it, he was just a welfare case they'd picked up. So he waved back at Konrad and walked away each time, including the last time, when he saw Konrad and Marta boarding a canvas-walled truck.

"So Saleh came through with the ransom?" he asked Manwar, who stood beside him with a Kalshnikoff in his hands.

"Part of it, yes, building materials and men to construct the first building, the library. Then I can move my books, once they have finished."

Manwar had collected quite a library, many of the volumes in English, a few in other non-Arabic languages, and an extensive collection of esoteric commentaries on the Quran. Three months after the new library is completed, a rival clan leader secretly in the employ of Manwar's Great-Uncle the Imam will shoot Manwar in the head, and all the books and the building holding them will be burned to the ground. The brick shell of the library will be canvassed over and used as a storehouse for weapons and ammunition and a small stash of Dutch porn magazines. But the day the tour group left, Manwar was excited, and he took Charlie to the hilltop to show him where the library, and the classrooms, and the gymnasium would eventually go.

"And it won't be another madrasah, though of course we will teach the words of Allah and his prophet Muhammed, if Allah wills it, but we will also teach dialectic and revolutionary theory and we will teach both genders, women too will learn, and I want to build a facility here for making solar panels, and over here a mosque, a humble mosque but beautiful, and over that hill, that flat place there is perfect for a health clinic, too small for a hospital but we are not many here..."

On the fourth day, Manwar took Charlie to a village nearby and led him to a bathhouse, handing him a square of linen and some rude smelling soap. He must have paid to rent out the entire bathhouse, Charlie thought, because I'm the only person inside. The water was warm and slightly oily and Charlie floated there a while, staring at the elaborate mosaic on the ceiling, at the places where tiles had fallen and been replaced, the places they had not been. It was here that Charlie first thought of staying in Yemen, that the bizarre chain of events that led him here was proof of a guiding hand, of Allah, sure, or God or Buddha or whatever, there had to be a reason and now he could see it: he was to stay here and help Manwar change the country. He'd already started to pick up some Yemeni words, the Yemeni Arabic that Manwar swore was more melodious than all the other Arabics, and he while he wasn't particularly handy, he could type, and do research, and be Manwar's secretary, his quiet collaborator. Why else would he begin one day in a motel in Pearson, Pennsylvania, and find himself a month later floating in a bathhouse in a village in the hinterlands of Yemen? The angels do indeed contemplate the infinite glory, Viktor was right, after all.

He got out and dried himself and dressed in the new robes Manwar had given him that morning. The main street of the village was lined with men sitting, reading the newspaper, resting behind carts of food and fabric and other goods they were selling, or taking elsewhere to sell, if they ever finished their qat-chewing. It was often siesta time in Yemen, Charlie thought, and I like that. Manwar appeared from around a corner of the building and opened his hands to Charlie. "Ah, you are freshly scrubbed, very good, come, we have business to attend to." Manwar's pickup truck waited around the same corner, Yasser and Na'em drowsily waving from beneath the tarp stretched over the bed. They drove back to the compound, where Manwar told Charlie to wait in his room, that they had special visitors coming, and that he should rest. When he woke he was famished, and Yasser brought him a plate of rice and bread and tea, grinning and nodding even more than usual. When Charlie was finished, he washed his hands in water Yasser poured from a jug, and allowed himself to be led into the courtyard, where Manwar stood waiting beside the truck, along with several older, elaborately dressed men Charlie didn't recognize. "Ah, here he is," Manwar said, guiding Charlie by the arm into the cab of the truck as the old men clambered into the bed. "Now we can talk about your future," he said to Charlie as he closed the door.

"Yes, I've been meaning to ask about that, if I could," Charlie replied.

"Of course," said Manwar.

"Well, I'm really excited about what you're trying to do here, and I feel, I don't know, like I'm meant to be here, so I want to... um, offer my services, I guess, maybe as your secretary or assistant or something, whatever job you think I might be good at, to help the revolution."

Manwar was silent for a few seconds, shifting gears and turning the car up the hill.

"You are going to help the revolution, of course. But you cannot stay here! What makes you think you can come here and help us!" His voice began to rise, and Charlie saw his hands were gripping the steering wheel whitely. "Another foreigner, here to save the poor Yemeni! I did not think you were such a reactionary. If you want to help, go tell your government to leave us alone, to stop propping up Saleh and his cronies, to stop—"

"I'm sorry, I'm sorry, I just thought—"

"You thought you would save us. Or perhaps you thought we could save you? You have your own people, we are not your people, we are all human beings, yes, but this is not your place. I knew you were not smart, but I did not think you a fool, Charlie Price."

They had reached the crest of the hill. At the top, Charlie saw two groups of people, thirty or forty yards apart. The group on the left were dressed in Yemeni clothes and huddled near an ancient Volvo panel truck and a few smaller cars and horses. The group on the right were clearly American, or perhaps European, a few wearing dark camos, a few in suits, all standing stiffly around a cluster of black SUVs, which in turn were circled around a massive yellow Hummer. Charlie half expected Big Al to pop out and ask how it was hanging. "What the..." Charlie put his hands on the dashboard and held on like he was aboard a roller coaster.

"Your future, Charlie. And I thank you for the help you have given us," Manwar said.

"Who are they?"

"Here, we have Al-Qaeda, our Yemeni chapter. Much bigger fools than you, but essential for bargaining. And over here, why, it is your people, Charlie. CIA, most likely, a few regular soldiers, perhaps, that one looks like Blackwater..." Manwar pointed at one of the men in black camo, staring at the Al-Qaeda camp. He was the only one on the American side who seemed to be paying them any attention.

"So what, why are they here?"

"To bid for you, of course."

"Bid? You're going, you're gonna sell me? To the highest bidder?" Charlie gripped the seat tightly.

"Of course," Manwar said. "Although the bidding is largely complete, at least the currency aspect. Both groups have offered us, hmmm," Manwar thought for a moment, "I think about twenty thousand dollars, the equivalent of that. You should be proud!"

"Proud? What the fuck!"

"Please, do not curse. I'm sorry for my outburst earlier, I have enjoyed our time together, but I can't understand why you think you are Yemeni now, after four days. Yes, you should be proud, your ransom is already the third highest offered for a single person. Now the sheiks will see what gifts they have brought, and decide."

"Gifts?"

"Gifts, yes, both sides have offered a very substantial amount of money, now they will show the sheiks what else they have to offer. Terrible, the materialism."

"Oh great, and then what? They kill me. Thanks a bunch, asshole," Charlie said, and Manwar's fist shot out and hit his jaw so hard his head smacked against the truck window.

"Please, no cursing. Yes, the Al-Qaeda will likely behead you, they are, most of them, congenitally retarded or mentally ill or otherwise people that their own families did not want. Many pedophiles, I hear, good thing you are not a boy anymore!" Manwar laughed and shook Charlie's shoulder. "On your side, I am not sure what will happen. Do you recognize those men? Are they from the prison?"

Charlie squinted. "I can't tell, I don't think so, but anyway they'll still kill me."

"Maybe, maybe not, but if so, I promise to make a poem about your martyrdom." Manwar was not laughing this time, and his earnest, stern glare told Charlie that he was not a radiant idealist, but another madman, one of many he had met in the past month.

"Come, we will see what gifts you earn us."

Manwar got out of the truck and went around to let Charlie out as well. "Wait here," He commanded, stationing Charlie a few feet in front of the truck. The old men had already jumped down from the pickup and were chattering loudly with the Al-Qaeda camp, while Manwar idled over to the American side. It was much hotter today than yesterday, Charlie thought. It never rains here, does it? Manwar walked over to the Al-Qaeda side and talked with the old men, then walked back to where Charlie was standing. "Your people are stupid and crass, but they drive a good bargain," he said.

"Yeah whatever, what's the deal?"

"Your people say that the money is reward enough, and they are right, but Al-Qaeda has brought us two fat goats and a large bale of qat. Of course, we grow qat in the valley, so it is not worth so much as they think. Very sturdy goats, though. I have no stomach for this materialism." He turned and rubbed his chin.

"Goats? Ok, can I talk to my people? Please?"

"No, of course not, when you go to buy milk, do the cartons speak to you and ask, 'buy me, I am the best'! No. Your side will bargain, I have told them what Al-Qaeda has offered."

The sheiks met Manwar in the center of the clearing and talked for a while, their gestures growing wilder, hands flaring out, spit flying. Manwar went back to the American side and spoke to one of the men in suits, then one of the soldiers got into the Hummer and started it, turning it around and backing it into the same spot. The man in the suit gestured to the sheiks, who gathered behind Manwar, standing now behind the back end of the Hummer. The suit threw open the tailgate and spoke, and Manwar translated, and the men all said ahh at once, chorally. Manwar took something the suit handed him and walked back toward Charlie, waving it, smiling.

"See! I told you your people bargained well, they are the masters of capitalism." He held out a small, white, flat card for Charlie to inspect. It looked a lot like an iPod.

"It looks like an iPod," Charlie said.

"It is one of five hundred iPods, actually. The elders are very impressed, though I don't think they really know what an iPod is, I told them they were microcomputers. And also, your people give us a case of frozen shark steaks," he gestured back toward the Hummer, "and also the big truck. The elders believe these are excellent gifts..." Manwar said, tilting his head to study the iPod. Charlie wondered where the ear buds were, but thought better than to mention it. He slumped back against the hood of Manwar's truck and watched the Al-Qaeda group slink back to their vehicles, muttering.

"Shark steaks? Did you really say shark steaks?"

"Yes, we do not have so much fish here in the north, and I don't think any of my people have ever tasted shark. It is a fearsome beast, so it must be a great delicacy, the sheiks believe. They truly are stupid old men. Have you eaten shark before?"

"No," Charlie replied, standing up as he saw the men in camo walking slowly toward him.

"Neither have I. I am more interested in the cooler the shark comes in, to be honest."

Charlie looked at the men in black camo. They could be twins, both block headed, pig-eyed, clean shaven, with protruding ears. "Guess I'm the prize," he said, and walked slowly, one man on each side, toward a waiting SUV. Every moment of his life spoke to him and told him to turn and tell Manwar to fuck off, but instead he plodded on, their chatter growing more joyous behind him, the bug-eyed sunglasses of the men in suits dissecting his stride.

CHAPTER 16

The way home was, like so many journeys, much easier than the way there. Not once was Charlie cuffed, or drugged, no bags were put on his head, no one punched him or stuck him in a broken walk-in cooler with a corpse. He was interrogated, endlessly, by people who looked as though they'd been punched out of a form: tightly clenched eyes, tightly clenched hair, walking with the gait of serious runners. And he answered them with the same story, until he found he could tell them what happened without actually thinking about what he was saying, letting his mind drift. He had a few serious bouts of diarrhea, and slept through most of the flight back to the States, which he suspected was on the same plane they'd first used to spirit him out of the country. At least his body told him so, the seats felt the same, the engines sounded the same, the rubbery arms of his seat were frayed at the ends where fingernails had dug into them. And then he was back in the United States, in Virginia, as Malcolm, his most frequent handler, told him. Climbing down from the plane onto the tarmac, the wind blew violently, and brought with it the unmistakable smell of french fries, and Charlie thought he could probably tell he was back home even if no one had told him, even if he had a bag on his head.

He was given a room in a large grey building at the end of a dull country road, hidden behind a thick swath of pine. The room was small, with a single bed, a chair, and a table with a short grey lamp, no windows, and a linoleum floor that looked as though it had been put in last week. Another clone of officialdom appeared, soon after he was deposited in his room, with a folded set of clothes, toiletries, and a piece of paper the clone used to trace the outline of

Charlie's sandals, wincing slightly at the smell of his infrequently washed feet. As he left, the man showed Charlie down the hall to a room with a toilet and shower, passing seven empty rooms as they walked. Charlie asked if he was the only person in the hall. "So far!" the clone glimmered, and escorted Charlie back to his room. After he left, Charlie tried the door to his room and found it open, then tried all three of the closed doors on the hall. The door to the bathroom was the only unlocked one. So, again, he was a prisoner, but at least he had no great fear of being shot in the head and dumped in a shallow grave, everyone was too nice, albeit in a clinical manner that suggested something worse than a head shot was distinct possibility.

Charlie took a shower and changed into his new clothes. A moment after he pulled on his socks, the same clone appeared at his door and knocked lightly before opening it. They must have cameras on me, that was way too quick, he thought. "Are you ready for lunch?" the man asked. He wore a tan, nondescript uniform that tried very hard to look unlike a uniform but failed. His hair was freshly cut, and he wore a spindly, sleek pair of glasses.

"Sure," Charlie answered, and the man led him through the locked door at the furthest end of the hall, down a long corridor made up of tall windows on one side that looked out on an elaborate garden. Several people dressed like the clone walked busily down the hall, but the garden was empty except for a tightly wound woman in a blue suit barking into a cell phone. "Where am I?" Charlie asked as they passed through a set of double doors into a large, busy cafeteria.

"You are in the Henry H. Goddard Center For the Study of Personal Values and Integrity, just outside of Fredericksburg, Virginia, and my name is also Charles, though I prefer to be called Charles and not Charlie, but if it makes you feel more comfortable to call me Charlie, knock yourself out! There are the trays, let's eat!"

Over the course of the next two days, Charles provided Charlie with anything he asked for, except when he didn't. A copy of *Down and Out in Paris and London* appeared six hours after he asked for it, but his request for a newspaper, any newspaper, was met with a knowing smile and "I'm sorry, not until the Doctor says it's ok" There was a media center next to the cafeteria with a good selection of fairly crappy books, and also individual televisions and headsets and a well-stocked library of DVDs, and Charlie spent much of his time there, but until the Doctor said it was ok, there would be no access to television or the internet. He was dissuaded from talking with other patients as well, although some of them seemed free to talk with one another—again, the Doctor, whoever that was, would someday grant him personal contact with someone other than Charles. Charlie felt very much like a lab rat, and he tried to spend as little time in his cell as possible.

It occurred to him that his present situation afforded him the space to reflect on what had happened to him, and why, and on the sort of person he had become, but he didn't, choosing instead to watch movies and read and generally try to avoid reflective thinking of any kind. If I'm going to be a rat in a cage, I might as well veg out, he told himself. Maybe aliens will come down and snatch me away, or I'll fall through the floor to the center of the earth and get eaten by dinosaurs. Who knows. This blasé attitude lasted until, on the second night, he lay down to sleep and was gripped with a panic that moved him to press the buzzer by the side of his bed and ask Amy, apparently the overnight clone in charge, for something to help him sleep. She brought him a small blue and white pill that worked so well he didn't rouse until Charles patted his cheek and yelled his name several times the following morning.

On the third day, Charles told him at breakfast he would meet the Doctor after lunch. He spent the time before lunch watching the *X-Men* movie, it was a crappy piece of fluff, and the guy they had playing Wolverine had only one facial expression in his repertoire. When he returned the DVD, he saw there was even a sequel in the rack. People will eat shit if you tell them it's candy, he decided, and went to join the Charles for lunch in the cafeteria.

"So, today is the day, huh?" he said to Charles, popping a french fry into his mouth.

"Yes, today you get to meet the Doctor! Excellent, she really is a great woman, I'm sure she'll help you get out of here asap." Charles only ever ate an iceberg lettuce salad with Italian dressing and chocolate milk.

"How did you end up here, Charles? Answer a job ad for prison guard slash life coach?"

"Ha ha, that's a good one. You know this isn't a prison, Charlie, we're just trying to help you. It will all make much more sense once you meet with the Doctor."

"Ok, but how did you get here?"

"I applied, of course. It's my job, and I get great satisfaction out of helping people too. Finding a job that fulfills you is the key to life, don't you think?"

"I guess so, I never had one, so I can't really say." He wiped his mouth and pushed the chair away. "So, it's your job, what would happen if I tried to run, or, like, get your keyring from you?"

"Ha, I don't think that would be in your best interest, but if that's what you need to do, knock yourself out!" Charles was half a foot taller than Charlie and he stood so as best to emphasize that fact.

"Nah, maybe later," Charlie answered, and they went out through a door in the back of the cafeteria that Charlie hadn't noticed before.

The Doctor's waiting room was small, with room for a reception desk and chair, a second chair facing the desk, and a small rack stuffed with copies of Sports Illustrated and Better Homes and Gardens. There was no receptionist, Charlie saw, and Charles pressed a button on the intercom that was the only thing on the desk.

"Yes?" came a tinny voice.

"Mr. Price here to see Doctor Martin," Charles answered.

"Very good, you can go, tell Mr. Price he can enter when he hears the buzzer."

"You can enter when—"

"I heard it, Charles, thanks," Charlie answered.

"Ok then, well, have a good talk, and I'll be back to get you when you're done. Oh, and to answer your question from lunch, I applied to work at the center as an intern while completing my Master's degree in clinical psychology at U Penn, and I fell in love with it. So, there you go, a little more knowledge to help you get your bearings." He smiled expectantly.

"That's great, Charles, thanks."

"No problemo, see you in a bit," he said, and left Charlie alone with the magazines and desk and intercom. He felt a great urge to press the intercom button and order a Happy Meal.

He also felt logy from his lunch, and the buzzer was loud enough to make jump. He stood and walked tentatively to the door, opened it a crack, and peeked through.

"Come," said a voice that reminded him of his Junior High gym teacher, Mr. Peebles. He went through the door and saw that the source of the voice was the tightly wound woman he had seen in the garden the day he arrived, and that she sat at a very large desk on the right side of the room. The left side of the room held a matching desk, where a meek looking woman sat pecking furiously at a computer keyboard.

"Name?" said the severe woman.

"Josh Tebow. Ha, no, just joking," he added quickly. "Charles Price. Charlie."

"Social Security number?"

"Oh wow, um..." the shapes of the numbers were there, but the numbers themselves avoided his grasp. "Uh, three six three, uh twelve, I'm having a hard time here."

"Three six three one two oh nine five six?" she said, reading from her computer screen.

"Yeah, that sounds right. Can you write that down for me?"

She peeled a bright orange post-it note from the stack on her desk and wrote it down for him.

"There you are, please go through the door ahead. Would you like any coffee or tea?"

"Yes, some tea would be nice, with sugar."

The meek woman pecked a few more times then stopped, got up, and slid by Charlie, who stood waiting for the tea.

"Marla will bring it to you, please go through the door."

"Oh, right," he answered, and went through the door.

The room on the other side did not belong in the same building Charlie just left. The wall facing him was a single, enormous wooden bookshelf, complete with a sliding ladder, all of it ornately carved like something from a men's club in the 1800s. The desk in front of the bookshelf was stainless steel and very sparsely covered, and the ceiling, which was at least twenty feet high, was hung with at least a dozen model airplanes, most of them biplanes. The wall to the right held a large window, bracketed by small pieces of abstract art, and the wall to the left was covered with framed photographs, hundreds of them. "Hello," a voice said, and Charlie realized a very tiny woman with a nest of grey hair atop a very large pair of glasses sat behind the desk.

"Hi," Charlie answered, unsure what to do next. These must be the aliens, he thought.

"Please, sit, please," she said, waving a bony hand toward one of two leather chairs in front of the desk.

"Oh, yeah, sorry," he answered, and sat, making the chair squeak angrily.

"My name is Doctor Martin, and you are," she glanced down at an open manila folder on her desk, "Charles Price?"

"Charlie?"

"Oh?" she replied, and made a mark on the paper with a small pencil, the kind used for scoring at miniature golf courses, Charlie noted.

"Yes. Charlie."

"Well. Charrrr-leee, my name is Doctor Martin, but you can call me Lily, though that's not my name," she said, erupting in giggles, "oh dear, I love that joke. My name is Cynthia." she stood and offered Charlie her hand, and he stood and shook it, then both sat down, his chair squeaking even louder. She looked back down at the folder and began to read, turning pages quickly.

"Well," she said, closing the folder.

"Uh, well, I guess you want to hear the story," he said.

"What story is that?"

"About how I got kidnapped and all that."

"Not really, maybe later. What I want you to do right now is to tell me what you are thinking."

He looked at the wall of photographs. "I'm wondering why I'm here."

"Good, that's a logical thing to think. Are you happy to be here?"

"Happy? Geez, I don't know, no, I'm not happy, I'm a prisoner," he said.

"Not exactly, but you are not yet ready to leave, so in one sense you are correct. The next question is: what, currently, are the positive aspects of your situation here?"

"You mean other than the prisoner part?"

174

"Is that a positive aspect of your situation?"

"No, of course not. Well, let me think..." he looked up at a model of a biplane with German markings from World War One. "Did you make these?"

"Yes, I did. Do you like models?"

"Sure, they're fine."

"I can provide you with tools to make your own, if you like," she said, sitting back in her chair.

"No, that's ok."

"Very well. Back to the question: what are some positive aspects of your present situation?"

"Ok, the food is free, but not very good, there are plenty of movies and books, though also not very good, I have a warm place to sleep..." he suddenly felt very squirrely, like he was tattling on a classmate in grade school.

"Excellent!" She shifted forward in her chair. "Finding the positive aspects of a given situation is the first step to health, and only by being healthy can you change your situation for the better. Here," she said, opening a drawer in the desk and pulling out a bright yellow piece of paper. "Please fill this out, it's a kind of survey, front and back." She handed him one of the little pencils from the cup full of them on her desk.

"A survey?"

"Yes, a survey to help you begin to assess your current happiness," she said.

"Happiness."

"Yes, happiness. Our goal here is to make you realize your potential for happiness. Not to make you happy, only to help you realize how happy you can be."

Charlie stared at her. "Happy?" He said again. "In the past I don't even know how long, I've been shot at, drugged, beaten, tied to a wheelchair, tortured repeatedly by what I think were Americans, fell down a cliff in fucking Yemen of all places, and then was sold to the CIA for twenty thousand dollars, some iPods, and a case of fucking shark steaks! You must know all this, it's in that goddamn folder, right? And then you ask if I'm happy? What the fuck."

A tiny, prim smile crept across her face. "Yes, you have had quite an adventure, haven't you?"

"Adventure? I was kidnapped! Twice! Three times, technically!"

"And how many young men, of your age and background, have managed to have such an adventure and live to tell the tale? Why, some people live their whole lives without dreaming of such excitement. Yes, I would say you are a very lucky young man, Charlie."

He stared at her in disbelief, feeling the color seep out of his face. "Ok, so the adventure's over, how do I get out of here and go back to my life?"

"The first step," she said, smile fading, "is to please fill out this form."

Charlie met with Dr. Martin every day after lunch, and it slowly dawned on him that he would never get out of the Center until she decided his 'happiness potential' was sufficiently robust. She was also hard to fool, he tried being sunny and bright for a while, and she grilled him in her bizarre way and gave him test after survey after test. At one session, she had him brought to a room in the basement where she hooked him to an EEG machine and asked him questions. On Halloween, she jumped out from behind her desk with a monster mask on as he came through the door. He told her what he thought she wanted to hear, made up all kinds of crazy stories about his childhood, and hoped he was doing better on the tests. She claimed to know nothing of the details of his internment, such as what happened to Dr. DeStefano, and refused to let him contact anyone from Pearson or read a newspaper, but he got a calendar and a clock radio and was allowed to watch a few television shows with the commercials removed, which reminded him how much he hated television programs. His sleeping pills were soon supplanted by a little cup of waking pills, and he had to admit they did make him more prone to seeing the positive aspects of things, and not get quite so anxious about his situation.

One day in mid-November, Dr. Martin called him to her office early in the morning and asked how he was getting on.

"Pretty good, thanks," he replied.

"I think so too, that's why I asked you here early. You've made good progress, so it's time for you to take another step."

"Ok, what?"

"For the next few days, I won't be meeting with you, because you need to absorb something, and see if you can find your own way. I will be ready to see you again on, ah—" she flipped the pages in a small appointment book, "Monday the twenty-second."

Charlie marked the date down in his own book, which matched hers.

"Ok, whatcha got?"

"Often, black swans enter our life. Do you remember discussing the black swans?"

"Yes, things sometimes happen that are out of our control."

"That's right, so I have a piece of news that will seem like a black swan, and it will threaten to darken your thoughts, but you must work through it."

Charlie stiffened, then nodded.

"Do you remember your keys to managing a Black Swan Event?"

"Not off the to of my head, no."

"That's ok, I've prepared a list for you." She slid a photocopy across the table to Charlie. He took it and watched the words squiggle blindly around the page.

"So. I am sorry to tell you, your mother has passed away, Charlie." She sat back and crossed her fingers.

"Is this another test?"

"No, I'm sorry, your mother passed away, she was in a car accident on the highway near her home. She died instantly, there was no pain."

Charlie started chewing the inside of his lip. "When did this happen?"

"September twentieth."

"September? What? And you tell me now?"

"You were not ready to deal with it before. Now, I believe, you are."

I will not cry in front of this woman, he thought. I will not give her the satisfaction.

"I would like to go back to my room now," he said.

"Of course, Charles will take you back." She smiled and tried to look empathetic

As he lay in bed that night, his sleeping pill dancing down the toilet stack, he resolved to get out of the Center as soon as he could, to play the game and act the way they wanted him to act but to never, ever, let go of the stony little nugget of hatred lodged in his chest. He would let it guide him, anchor him as he played his role, for the angels lost in perpetual contemplation of infinite glory knew that there was hatred in that glory, and rage, and revenge. Right now, revenge meant getting away, and getting away with it.

Thanksgiving passed, and Christmas, and then it was 2005 and he was allowed to read the newspapers, where he discovered that a horrible earthquake off the coast of India had caused a tsunami, that Sprint bought Nextel, that there were still wars in Iraq and Afghanistan, that the Cardinals won the World Series, and that apparently Bush had been re-elected. He didn't ask for a newspaper again after that, but did spend the odd hour surfing the internet, mostly studying maps, which he found oddly comforting. He lost hours staring at old maps archived at various sites, and also playing a map-heavy video-game called *Civilization III* that someone had thoughtfully loaded into the computer.

In early January, Dr. Martin told him he would be ready to leave soon.

"Great, I'm looking forward to getting back home."

"Yes, that's what we have to discuss. I would like someone to join me, if that's alright with you, he can explain better than I what comes next."

"Ok, fine," Charlie agreed. Dr. Martin pressed the intercom buzzer, and a few seconds later the door behind them opened. "Please come in, Mister Danko," she said, and a cleanly dressed man with a very expensive watch was shaking Charlie's hand. The pills in his daily cup had changed in the last few days, and he found it difficult to focus his vision widely, preferring to stare at what was close in front of him. The man's face was huge, and Charlie looked at the floor after they stopped shaking.

"Charlie, this is Mister Danko, he is a U. S. Marshall."

"Hello Charlie," Danko said.

"Hi."

"Mister Danko will tell you about the next step, and I will try to help fill in where I can," Martin said.

"Ok."

"Charlie," Danko said sliding into the chair beside him, "you've been through a lot, I hear."

"Yep, I got myself into quite a mess, it's good to be home."

"I bet it is. Now, where to start..." he sat back and tapped his fingers together, and Charlie saw the pistol in his belt. "You know we're at war, correct?"

"Yes, two of them, actually, so we're at wars, I guess."

"That is correct, yes, and the real war is, of course, the war on terror. Now, this war is hard to fight, because our enemies can be anywhere. The real war is for information, for information about where our enemies are, and to keep our own information hidden from them, and from people sympathetic to them. Make sense?"

"Yes, but you could be a little more specific," Charlie said.

"Specifically, you are the source of certain information that could be dangerous to our way of life."

Charlie looked at his shoes, one of which had a large scuff. "I'm not following you."

"The, ah, unfortunate series of incidents that you were part of could be very damaging to our image, and to our soldiers and our other operatives overseas."

Charlie cocked his head. "So, you don't want me to tell?"

"Well, yes, that's one way to say it, and we don't want anyone to know that you, well, that you are who you are. There are people out there who know who you are, and they would like to get their hands on you, I promise you that." He shifted forward in his seat. "We need to ensure your safety, so that we can ensure our great nation's safety."

Sensing he was overdoing it, Dr. Martin interjected. "What I believe Mister Danko is offering, Charlie, is an opportunity, an opportunity for a whole new life."

"Really? How so?" He scratched his nose and looked sideways at Danko.

"Have you heard of the Witness Protection Program, Charlie?"

"Sure, I never believed it was real, though."

"Oh, it's very real. But what we have in mind for you is a kind of offshoot of that program, one that will keep you safe for a very long time."

"Ok, what does it mean? Do I have to stay here? I mean, it's nice here," he smiled at Dr. Martin, "but I'd kinda like to get back to my life."

"A new life, Charlie, that's the beauty of it. How many people get a chance for a new life?" Dr. Martin said. The idea of starting a new life would in fact germinate within her at this very moment, and would grow to obsess her until she left the Center nine months later to move to Belize and paint portraits of local children.

"That's true... how does it work?"

"Well," Danko leaned back again, "you have your choice of re-location sites, from a list we provide, of course. We provide you with a new identity, a home, and a stipend, and all you have to do is sign a contract promising, well, promising to keep your sensitive information under your hat, so to speak."

"And what if I didn't? I mean, what if I just said yes and then went to the newspapers or something?"

"That, Charlie," said Dr. Martin as Danko's eyes narrowed, "would not be in your best interests."

Charlie thought for a minute, looking at his nails, which seemed very far away.

"Ok, but I also want my degree," he said, finally.

"I'm sorry?" Said Danko.

"My bachelor's degree, from an accredited college. In Political Science. I never did finish, and it will help me get a job."

"You won't need a job—"

"I think a job would help Charlie very much, perhaps something part-time to start," Martin interjected. "And, there will be another person for you to see and talk with, like you do with me, at whatever site you choose."

"And I get a bachelor's degree, in Political Science, from an ac-credited university."

Danko sighed. He stared at the ceiling for a moment, then shook his head. "Yes, I think we can manage that, we can get you your degree."

"Excellent, where do I sign?" Charlie said, smiling lopsidedly. Danko smiled too, and the exertion nearly broke his head in half. It took the sight of his first child, born a few years later, to teach him how to smile in earnest, and her teenage descent into drug addiction and prostitution was enough to ensure that he never smiled again thereafter. Charlie's smile stayed with him all the way back to his room, where he finally put it all together: the whole journey was his internship, like working at the Center was for Charles, a strenuous, unpaid learning experience with a job at the end of it. Mom would be proud.

CHAPTER 17

The first time everything changed for Jim Rivers, he was sitting in his condo in Bricktown, minding his own business. That was, more or less, his vocation, which bothered his girlfriend, Summer, to no end, as she was committed to stopping the war, eradicating poverty, impeaching the President, and whatever other progressive causes she could find to rally around in Oklahoma City, which was proving a lonely place to express such commitments. He wanted to help, and gave money to all sorts of organizations she supported, talked through the issues with her, and even helped design fliers for rallies, but he flatly refused to participate in any action, insisting that his job would be in jeopardy if he did. "And what is it you do again?" was her normal response to this, and he would remind her they had already discussed this, and here, try this new weed he got from Kinky, and then they would make furious love or watch a movie and that was that.

It was not a bad life, except for the fact that he really didn't have a job, other than minding his own business, and a few half-assed online ventures he'd started, like the build-your-own t-shirt site and the mix-your-own freezy pop site and the one that would make welcome mats from your family photos. He had a knack for investing, or was at least lucky, and had built himself a small but vigorous portfolio using the crumbs of his monthly stipend. None of these things sufficiently occupied his time, however, as he confided to his therapist, Dr. Hinckley, who responded by upping his Prozac scrip, which was Dr. Hinckley's response to whatever meager trauma Jim brought him, like a child at confession scrabbling to catalogue his sins, any sins. Jim had long since stopped taking all the different pills Hinckley provided him, preferring marijuana and bottles of moderately priced wine and giving the pills to Summer to dispense to friends, the homeless, whoever.

And then it all changed, on a day in late August, as he was minding his own business, staying in the air conditioning while Oklahoma City broiled. Tired of playing *Alpha Centauri*, he opened his internet browser and his home page, the *Pearson Sentinel*, popped into view. A sidebar headline caught his eye: "Detective Killed In Single Car Crash," and he followed the link to read how Detective Shinevsky had fallen asleep at the wheel on his way to an overnight shift and plowed over an embankment. The sight of the name, and the photo of the back of his car sticking out over the embankment, made Jim think about how he'd lost his mother—it could even have been the same embankment—and he started to twitch. He got up and did a few bong hits to calm himself, then went back to the computer. Beside the photo of Shinevsky's car was an ad for "Cavuto Motors," and the twitch started again. Fucking weird, he thought, just a fucking weird coincidence, I need to stop reading this shit anyway, it's all in the past, a past that never was.

He changed the page to national news, burrowing quickly into the sports page to avoid the malignancy of the front matter. Well hell, the Phillies lost, they were only a few games behind the Braves and had looked strong during the game he'd watched on Tuesday. He scanned the box score, went back to the main sports page, and noticed the ticker scrolling at the bottom: "Wolverine Injured." They're reporting on the X-Men in the sports page now, he thought, and followed the link to read about Jake Long, star offensive tackle of the University of Michigan's football team, who'd gotten his leg tangled up with another player; he'd be out for a month or two at least. Jim heard a clicking noise coming from somewhere and darted his eyes around the room. The noise grew louder, he rose from his chair and navigated each room, but the noise stayed at the same volume wherever he went, and he realized it was coming from his jaw, that he was grinding his teeth. The Wolverines? He stood beside his bed and stared out the window. The University of Michigan's team name is the Wolverines? How did I not know that? Manwar, Beth, the X-Men movie at the center, Cavuto Motors—the whole thing was a fucking set-up, and now someone was taunting him. No, not someone: Derek Cavuto.

Get a hold of yourself, Charlie, he said to himself. No, Jim, you are Jim now, get a hold of yourself, Josh, Jim, what the fuck. He went to the hall and got on the elevator, hoping a blast of heat and maybe a cappuccino would shake him back to his senses. The heat did indeed blast, a gritty gust of hot wind welcoming him as he stepped to the front of the building and started around the block. It's all this weed I've been smoking, he thought, I'm just getting creepy paranoid, need to just dry out for a while and get my bearings.

He didn't notice the ice cream truck when it first came around the corner, but then he heard it, and then he saw it, and he stood in the street in front of it and put his hand out like a traffic cop. The truck slowed, and Jim went around to the side. "What can I do ya for," said the driver, and Charlie stared. If it wasn't Skeech, the bastard who had twisted his nipples with a pair of pliers in a some warehouse in Pearson, then it was his brother, right down to the missing front tooth and birdish head movements. "Uh, hey," he answered.

"Hey yourself, hot one, huh?" the driver answered.

"Yeah, hot—hey, what song is that?"

"What?"

"The song your truck plays, what is it?"

The driver's eyes widened. "The fuck if I know, man, what are you, tripping?"

"It's 'Turkey In The Straw', motherfucker! That's what it is!" Charlie yelled, pointing his finger in the driver's face.

"Great, boss, good for you," said the driver, ducking quickly into the front of the truck and screeching away. Charlie stood in the middle of the street for a few seconds, then went back into his condo to pack.

The note he left in Summer's mailbox was vague, a little cryptic even, but, he thought, sufficient: Hey babe, got a shitstorm at the main office, I need to fly out there and take care of things. I should be back in a few days, I really care about you a lot, you know? If anything weird happens, just remember that I love you. It was a little over the top, he thought, but so be it, she was a good woman and deserved a much better man than him. He wasn't flying, that would be too easy to trace, instead tossing a suitcase into the back of his Corrolla and getting on the interstate. Twelve hours later he was in Indiana, flipping the channels in a Motel 6, wondering what he would do when he got to Pearson.

The next morning before getting back on the highway he stopped at a hardware store to buy the things he needed, the things he'd listed out the night before: paint thinner, a box of razors, duct tape, twenty feet of rope, a small axe, a hammer, and the largest nails he could find. He stopped at the knife display, fascinated by the multiplicity of shapes and gleaming blades, and bought as well a seven inch CKRT fixed blade survival knife, which cost as much as the rest of his items put together. Supplies secure in the trunk, he rejoined the interstate, enjoying the light sway of the hills, the scrubby trees waving from the highway, the broken barns sagging in on themselves, the changing accents on the radio. I am going to take from him what he took from me, and more, he told himself, imagining Cavuto's face as he felt the nails going into his body, the knife opening his flesh just like the blade had opened Charlie, all over his body, tiny cuts and vinegar—it would be some homecoming. Damn, if only he hadn't forgotten his camera.

Pearson looked like a dream he'd had, like the ghosts of buildings too stupid to die were lingering in a valley to worn out to consume them. He drove aimlessly through the darkened streets, wandering past the college, suddenly finding himself in front of his Mom's house. Some kind of stock car sat in the front yard up on blocks, the number 47 painted on the side, and all the windows in the house were lit. He sat a while listening to his mind whir and click, then pulled out and drove to his old apartment. The street looked the same, as did his house, and he parked at the curb and got out. The hole where Cavuto shot at him was still there in the siding, and he reached up on his tip-toes and ran his fingers over it. The edges were smooth, word already by wind and rain, and he put a finger in the hole and pulled and a large chunk of siding came off and hit him on the arm as he tried to jump clear.

"You! Craven boy!" someone barked.

"What?" He turned and saw a small head poking out of the window to his left.

"They been looking for you, everybody been looking then they stop, they know you craven and worthless. Now you get away from there, duppy! Go on!"

Charlie backed away from the house, nodding at the head. He drove on to the ice cream truck dispatch yard, but it appeared abandoned. Cavuto Motors, right; he needed a better plan, enough wandering around. The motel where he'd met Beth was still open, so he got a room, bought a map of Pearson at the convenience store, and started marking it.

He rose before sunrise and drove to Cavuto's house, parking down the street behind another car. Just as the sun came up, a door opened and there he was, the same stupid haircut, though Charlie was surprised to see he wearing a rumpled suit and not a wife-beater and jeans. Charlie watched as Cavuto kissed a smallish woman who wore a head wrap of some kind, got in a late model BMW, and drove off. Rather than follow him, Charlie waited, and soon the woman re-emerged, each hand holding the hand of a young girl. They walked to the end of the driveway and then up to the corner, where a school bus appeared: the girls boarded and the woman waved, and Charlie pulled away from the curve, driving slowly to see what kind of woman would marry a monster. She looked tired, her body slumping noticeably once the bus had pulled away and she started walking back. Her face was very pale, her nose narrow, her eyebrows painted on crookedly. Not at all worth it, Charlie thought, she looks half dead already.

He continued on and decided to follow the school bus, which ended up at Robert E. Perry elementary, where Charlie had gone to school and where his mother had taught all her life. It looked dingier than he remembered, though the basketball nets looked brand new. He watched as Cavuto's children got off the bus, snapping a few pictures of them with his camera phone, then pulled away to find Cavuto Motors, on Blasdell street.

The auto dealership was a great disappointment, shitty used cars covered with flags and banners, a single trailer sitting in the middle of the yard. Haven't done so well for yourself, Charlie laughed, in fact this place is a fucking joke. He sat most of the morning in the Pump-n-Pantry across from the yard, getting out at noon to buy a microwave burrito and a Coke. While waiting for the microwave to ding, the door to the store opened and Charlie heard a voice he knew:

"Hiya Boss, how's it hanging?" He turned his head slightly and saw Cavuto's back in front of the register. "Lemme get a pack of Camel's and pay ya tomorrow, alright?"

"You still owe me thirty five dollars and seventeen cents, you must pay your bill before I let you have anything else," said the mustached man behind the register.

"Oh come on, Habib, you know I'm good, I just need to sell a few of these babies, things are slow right now."

"Thirty five dollars and seventeen cents."

Charlie saw Cavuto's shoulders drop. "Ok, ok..." he said, and walked slowly out of the shop. The microwave dinged, and Charlie laid his burrito gingerly on a small stack of napkins. Cavuto was across the street by the time Charlie finally left the store, and he disappeared into the trailer as Charlie settled in behind the steering wheel. This was not part of the plan, what was the fun of torturing your arch-nemesis to death if he wasn't scary? He not only wasn't scary, I actually feel bad for him, no no no this is not how it's supposed to happen. Killing his wife would be a fucking favor, hell, killing you would be a fucking favor, by the look of things, what happened, chief? Where's the tough guy routine, the dead dogs gutted in people's trucks, where are all your wannabe gangster buddies? No, this is part of the trick, it's all part of the setup, you took my life away, you took my name, for fuck's sake, maybe you even took my mother, maybe you had something to do with her 'crash' maybe not, who knows, I didn't even get to go to the funeral. I am here to set things right, to restore balance and make the temperature of the planet stable again, make the sun keep moving and the clouds keep floating along and so, and so, like begets like. I know what is just, I know what must be done in the name of justice.

Charlie pulled up to the school and waited in the car. His head was on fire, he had tried to plan it quickly, as he drove: tie them both up, put something over their mouths, duct tape, then cut them, or maybe hit them both with the hammer first so they don't make noise, so they don't feel it, then the arms first? Would his knife cut through bone? Would he have to carve around the bone? Ok, just hit them with the hammer, dump the bodies on the stoop with a note. Maybe carve something into their skin, 'For Miriam,' or no, something to throw the cops off the trail, 'Butcher of Pearson', no, that's stupid... how to get them from the car to the hotel room? I need a tub for the blood, or maybe the woods, Jesus this was confusing, he thought. The bell rang and the children spilled out, a flood of children, he panicked, he would never find them, and then there was the smaller girl, talking to some friends, no sign of the taller one, he watched as she waved to the other girls and headed down the walk toward her bus. He pulled the car up behind the last bus and jumped out and waved at her, waved again and she didn't notice so one more time and yes, he caught her eye, suspicious, and he smiled a big sunny smile and walked slowly toward her. "Hey, it's ok, I'm a friend of your dad's, a friend of Derek's, he said to come get you."

"I don't know you," she said, backing away.

"I'm Jim, didn't Derek, I mean your Dad, say I'd be coming to get you?"

"Nuh-uh," she answered.

"Ok, well, I'm visiting from out of town and I volunteered to take you all to Chuck E. Cheese, where's your sister, anyway?"

"She got in trouble again, she has to stay after."

"Oh. That's too bad. I used to get in trouble a lot too. Well, ok, you can take the bus, you can't be too careful, just tell your Dad you were scared. I'm going to your house now, guess I'll see you there later," he said, and walked back to the car. As he opened the door, he saw her standing on the other side of the car.

"How do you know my Dad?"

"Derek? I actually knew your Mom first, um, Sylvia, then I met Derek when they started dating."

"Mom's sick," the girl said.

"Yeah, yeah, I know, that's why I'm here, to cheer her up."

"You can't cheer her up, she's gonna die, Billie says."

"Well, yeah, everybody dies, but—"

"No, Billie says she's gonna die soon, that's why all her hair is gone, and some of the sixth-graders tease Billie about it and she gets mad and punches them in the mouth. That's why she's in trouble."

Charlie stared at her pouting lip, her dark blue eyes, the clump of something, maybe peanut butter, lodged in her hair, the "Hello Kitty" lunchbox, and he tried to imagine hitting her in the head with a hammer. He tried to picture Cavuto's face on her body... "Hey, Angie, you get away from there!" someone yelled, and Charlie saw the older girl loping across the lawn. Angie turned and started to back away from the car.

"It's ok Billie, I'm a friend of your Dad's," Charlie said, holding his hands out before him, palms up.

"I never seen you before," she said, face pinched with fury.

"He's gonna take us to Chuck E. Cheese," Angie said.

"He's a fucking creeper, that's who he is," Billie said, shoving Angie behind her.

"No, no, I'm not a creeper..." Charlie felt the earth shifting beneath him. He grabbed the car to steady himself.

"I never seen you, go away or I'll scream!"

"Ok, ok sorry, look, just tell your Dad something for me, ok? Will you do that?"

Billie looked around the yard. A few more kids had piled out of the school, the buses were gone, and a few cars stood idling in the circle. "Ok, what?"

"Just tell him I'm sorry, tell him Charlie was by, Charlie Price, and that I'm sorry. Can you remember that?"

"Do I look stupid?"

"No," he answered, opening the car door. "No, you don't look stupid. You look—really brave."

He pulled out of the row of cars, out of the bus circle, and out of Pearson, back onto the interstate. The sky was clear and as blue as the ocean, the ocean he remembered his Mom taking him to, just the two of them for his ninth birthday, and he got sunburned and shit on by a seagull and tasted saltwater and she fell asleep and he heard her snore, he stopped digging a hole in the sand and looked out at the water and the sky, an undivided blue as far as he could see, and he knew what beauty was, and that it was infinite. The road back to Oklahoma City did not stop in Oklahoma City, he thought; none of the roads ever stopped, nothing ever did, we just pretend, just like I'll pretend, in a few days, when I'm on the couch with my arm around Summer watching some crap movie, that I'm not hurtling through space, that I'm more than a sudden flare of energy fading back into the fabric of time. He turned the driver's side window down to feel the hot air push against his face, and decided to get off at the next exit to try and find an ice cream sandwich.

www.ingramcontent.com/pod-product-compliance
Lightning Source LLC
Chambersburg PA
CBHW071911220626
47052CB00002B/302